A

Elaine Meyers has worked with books and stories
as a librarian, storyteller and writer. She lives in
Upstate New York with her husband and continues
to tell stories and share books with her four
grandchildren and local students. *Iron Pants* is a
fictionalized account of her mother's life.

IRON PANTS

ELAINE MEYERS

IRON PANTS

Vanguard Press

VANGUARD

PAPERBACK © Copyright

2022

Elaine Meyers

The right of Elaine Meyers to be identified as author of
this work has been asserted by her in accordance with the
Copyright, Designs and Patents Act 1988.

A CIP catalogue record for this title is
available from the British Library.

ISBN 978 1 80016 152 8

*Vanguard Press is an imprint of
Pegasus Elliot MacKenzie Publishers Ltd.*
www.pegasuspublishers.com

First Published in 2022

**Vanguard Press
Sheraton House Castle Park
Cambridge England**

Printed & Bound in Great Britain

Dedication

To Tom, my man for others and for life

Acknowledgements

To those who understand that schools are places of learning, affirmation, and joy.

My thanks to Dr Martin Luther Kesler, Patricia Carlton, Marian Rubach, Patricia Tatspaugh, and Patrick Jensen.

To all the librarians who help students find just the right books at the right time and provide the places and opportunities for individual growth.

My thanks to Minnie Elmer, Martha Makosky, Gail Griffith, Eleanor Jo Rodger, Ralph Edwards, Toni Garvey and Virginia Walter.

To fellow writers who understand the process and purpose of staying in the chair.

My thanks to Syracuse YMCA's Downtown Writers Center, Bill Castle Trio, Deb Hoke, Ellen Schmidt, and the two with me from the beginning, my invaluable colleagues Judith Pratt and Susan Trausch.

To my friends who read, encouraged, and advised. My thanks to Peter Tosto, Patricia Coggin, Arline Clair, the Gloss Family, Janet Heslop, Sydney Hasenjager,

Paul Mitchell, Sharon Rao, Nynette Adams and David Pierce.

Lastly, and most importantly, to my family where my deepest comforts and iron love abide. To Tom, Tim and Cheryl, Katie and David, Jackson, Claire, Emily and Laine.

No one can make you feel inferior without your consent.
Eleanor Roosevelt

Preface

My mother, Josephine, was an orphan—something she kept hidden. It was more a secret than a treasure. Her closest friends did not know. When we visited her sisters, I never heard them talk about their parents or their childhood. I knew she was an orphan because I was a relentless child who pursued my questions, even when it was clear my mother would rather not talk. She loved me more than her discomfort.

As I imagine my mother's youth, I see a misty bridge. On the bridge are four girls ages fifteen, thirteen, ten and four. They are joined by an older father who cannot read or write. At his side stands a much beloved mother with long auburn hair, blue eyes and a Bible in her hand. She is the second wife, and the mother of the four girls.

Beyond this bridge in central Appalachia stands a cabin. I can't see its shape or contents. Eventually there will be two coffins leaving this homestead for the Zion Cemetery—the fathers in 1915, and the mothers in 1918. Four orphan girls will stand together as the coffins disappear into the earth. Without parents, they cling to each other for family and strength.

I attack the mist with my pen and imagination. As I write, a name appears on the page—Iron Pants. Iron is the most common element on Earth. Iron isn't the strongest metal, but it is in our blood and makes us strong. Iron is shaped by fire. Iron Pants is the name my mother calls herself. Life provides Mother many challenges—poverty, tuberculosis, death, war and family separations. Iron Pants uses honesty, courage and stories to stand her ground and hold on to those she loves. You must be strong to love and be loved. If you are a loving daughter, you will always carry your mother with you—something that Elaine and Josephine share.

The mist clears and I begin to write.

PART 1

Chapter 1: Orphans

Today, my friend Susie and I had lunch with her mother-in-law, Mrs Scott. I was surprised when Mrs Scott, who hardly ever spoke, told this story:

When Jeffrey was just two years old, Mr Scott and I brought him to this very restaurant for an ice cream. Jeffrey was such a verbal child. He ate his ice cream and recited the name of every flavor he knew— chocolate, strawberry, vanilla, mint, sherbet.

After we finished, we waited in line to pay our bill. Jeffrey pointed to a jar filled with coins and dollar bills that sat on the desk near the register. "Whose money?" he asked.

I always wanted to encourage Jeffrey's interest in words. I pointed to the sign next to the jar and read. "Please help our church serve the orphans in foreign lands. Any contribution will help."

Jeffrey looked at me. "What is an orphan?"

"An orphan is someone whose mother and father have died."

Jeffrey's eyes got wide. His face twisted in surprise, changed to horror, and then grief. He began to cry and then wail. He put his head on my shoulder and would not let go of me. He cried for almost an hour.

Mrs Scott ended her story. "Who would believe that a two-year-old could understand the real meaning of being an orphan? Who would think that one so young would understand the bond between mother, father and child?"

Let my mother's story begin.

Warren County North Carolina
Spring 1918

Ten-year-old Josephine sighed, blinked her blue eyes, and gazed out the window as the cold wind whistled and shook the front door. She wore yesterday's old blue sack dress, and her straight reddish-brown hair was slowly coming unbraided. Her job was to watch and listen for the doctor. Her mother's life depended on the doctor arriving on time.

The rain had smeared the dirt on the glass, the frame needed paint and the ledge was dusty. She longed to see signs of spring, not the mist rising from the valley spreading gray in its wake. Mother said it wasn't spring until the dogwood bloomed. Where was the doctor?

The sound of labored breathing made her look from her post at the window to her mother's bed in the center of their small cabin home. Mother's auburn hair was tangled, and her face buried in a worn bedsheet. Her sharp shoulder bones and curved spine shaped the two thin and faded brown blankets covering her wasted body.

Josephine remembered how her oldest sister, fifteen-year-old Betty, had tried to change the bedding last week. Mother groaned when she was touched. Betty cried as she took the clean sheets back to the closet. Mother's Bible lay on a small table near the bed. The table was empty except for the Good Book and Mother's hairbrush.

Today, Betty stood by Mother's bed with her arm around thirteen-year-old Pamela. Like Josephine, her older sisters hadn't changed their clothes. Betty wore an old brown smock but had combed her light brown hair and tied it back with a ribbon. Pamela had pulled an old dress over her faded flannel nightgown and hadn't brushed her hair in two days. Four-year-old Nora Ann had dressed herself when she woke up. She was the only one wearing fresh clothes. She had brushed her hair but refused to let Betty braid it.

Looking at Mother made Nora Ann cry. Nora Ann lay at the foot of Mother's bed and had cried herself to sleep.

Josephine left the window and joined her sisters. Betty whispered, "You know that our Mother is very, very ill. Our dear minister Reverend Miller is on his way with a friend—Doctor Stevens from the Asheville tuberculosis clinic. Prayers and medicine might work, but we must prepare for the worst."

"No, no, no…" Josephine whispered. The NO in her head was screaming and rattling her skull. She understood Betty's words, but her heart refused to believe. Josephine straightened her shoulders, "Betty, you can call for all the help you want, but I know the truth. Mother loves us too much to die. You can stop right now!"

Betty shook her head and put a finger to her lips. "Josephine, please, you'll wake Nora Ann."

Pamela glared at Betty and Josephine. "You'll both wake her. Your words aren't changing anything. I think we have all known the worst could happen, Betty. I hope Reverend Miller and his friend Doctor Stevens will save us." Pamela rubbed her hands. Her eyes were filled with sadness.

Josephine moved to the hearth, adding the last log to the smoldering fire. "I'm going out for more wood. Mother needs to be warm to get well." As she stomped out of the cabin, her eyes fell on the dwindling woodpile at the bottom of the front porch. Where would she get more wood? She loaded her arms and glared at Betty who stood holding the door open. "It's all right Betty. When Mother gets well, we will all feel better."

Betty sighed, "Josephine, I want our Mother well. But sometimes, we need to see what is right in front of us. Thank you for the wood. We all need the warmth."

After Josephine stoked the fire, the room began to warm. Betty put the kettle over the fire. All they had was tea and bread from their neighbors. Pamela gently woke Nora Ann. "Mother wants us to eat now, Nora Ann. You can snuggle again after lunch." The sisters waited for the water to boil and toasted their bread over the fire. Nora Ann kept twisting around and looking at Mother.

Josephine followed her gaze. Mother had not moved, opened her eyes or said a word in the past two days. Her rattling breath was like a song that played day and night. Josephine gave Nora Ann a hug and moved her chair closer. Maybe a story would help soothe Nora Ann. Her eyes fell to the rug in front of the fireplace.

"Nora Ann, have I ever told you the story about this rug?" Nora Ann shook her head no and snuggled closer as Josephine began. "After Daddy died, Mother gathered all his old clothes and put them in a basket near her bed. One day, she said, 'I think your Daddy wants you to have a rug made of these old clothes. But it won't be just any rug. It will be the rug where you sit when we tell stories. Daddy wants you to remember that stories can be funny as well as sad.'"

Josephine was about to tell Nora Ann how it had sounded when Mother made the rug ripping rags, coughing, ripping rags and coughing. She was going to say how brave Mother was when she realized she did not want to tell a sad story.

How would her Daddy end the story? She smiled and let Daddy finish the tale: "So Mother ripped the clothes and braided the rug. When she put it by the fire, Mother straightened her shoulders and imitated Daddy's voice saying 'Make do with what you have. This rug proves you can be both tough and pretty. With your mother around there will always be a story hidden in everything we love.'"

As she finished the story, Josephine realized that both Betty and Pamela were listening. They both smiled and Betty said, "Time for some tea." She poured a cup of tea for Pamela and Josephine and got a glass of water for Nora Ann. Everyone nibbled their toast and quietly sipped their drinks. They longed to hear Mother tell a story again—what good was a story rug without a storyteller?

Josephine broke the silence, "When are Reverend Miller and Doctor Stevens going to get here? Betty, we need a doctor now!"

Betty tried to straighten her shoulders as she turned to her sisters. "When Reverend Miller visited Mother last week, he said he would pick up Doctor Stevens at the Norlina train station today. He had to borrow a carriage and mare from the Reilly family to make sure they could transport everything the doctor needed. I am sure they are coming as quickly as they can."

Josephine's eyes widened, "What, that old mare! She can hardly pull the Reilly's hay wagon! It will take them all day in that rickety wagon with that ancient horse. What good are fancy new medicines if they depend on the worst horse and wagon in the Appalachian Mountains?" Josephine clenched her hands.

Pamela cried, "I think I hear them!"

The four sisters ran out on the porch. In the distance, they saw Reverend Miller riding an old swaybacked horse, and his friend Doctor Stevens driving a wagon pulled by the sagging Reilly mare. The mist and wind made them dreamlike as they weaved along the mountain path leading up to the cabin. It seemed to Josephine that the old mare could barely lift her hooves, let alone pull a wagon.

Josephine realized that the Reilly mare fit right in with the Duke farm. Their garden was overgrown with weeds, and only the big stems of the rhubarb promised any nourishment. Everything needed paint—barn, cabin, fences, and porch.

She watched the one piece of furniture on the porch—an old rocking chair with a broken arm rest—swing in the wind like a ghost was rocking. *Swing Low Sweet Chariot* started playing in Josephine's head. She was startled when Pamela began to sing:

I looked over Jordan and what did I see?
Comin' for to carry me home.
A band of angels, a-comin after me,
Comin' for to carry me home.
Swing low, sweet chariot, Comin' for to carry me home.
Swing low, sweet chariot, Comin' for to carry me home.

Josephine and Pamela sang until Nora Ann began to shiver. Pamela took her inside. Betty and Josephine waited on the porch, watching the horses and wagon pass the fields, garden and barn. Finally, the wagon pulled up. The men dismounted and tied their horses to the front railing. Josephine was surprised to see a big trunk in the bed of the Reilly's wagon.

"Sorry we're late, Betty," apologized Reverend Miller. "Here, Doctor Stevens, let me help you with your bag."

Reverend Miller was looking more mountain-threadbare with each visit. His friend Doctor Stevens looked very rich in his nice wool suit and fancy leather bag with the brass fittings.

Doctor Stevens didn't waste time. He nodded at Josephine and Betty as he went through the front door. Inside he smiled at Nora Ann and Pamela standing by the fire and went to Mother's bed.

The four sisters followed. Josephine cleared her throat and stepped closer to the doctor. "Mother hasn't said anything or opened her eyes for two days. When we kiss her, she doesn't smile any more. We love her and need her. You must make her well, Doctor Stevens. She wants to be our mother."

Josephine knelt by the bed and grabbed her mother's hand.

"Let me see," said Doctor Stevens. He took Mother's other hand and felt her wrist for a pulse. He took his stethoscope and listened to her lungs.

The doctor's face told a story Josephine could not bear. "Where are your medicines that will make our mother well?" Doctor Stevens put up his hand. It was hard to hear a heartbeat with Josephine yelling.

Betty moved closer to the foot of Mother's bed without looking at Josephine or Doctor Stevens—her eyes on Mother. Nora Ann lay down on the bed. Pamela knelt by Josephine. As he removed his stethoscope,

Doctor Stevens raised his eyes to Reverend Miller and shook his head. Pamela's face went white.

Reverend Miller closed his eyes and then looked up. "Girls, bow your heads and let us pray. What was the prayer that your mother loved and taught you?"

"No, no, no! The doctor came to make Mother well. We don't need to pray. We need our mother." Tears fell down Josephine's cheeks as she tightened her grip on Mother's hand. Reverend Miller moved closer and put his hand on her shoulder. Slowly he began to sing:

> *Amazing Grace, how sweet the sound,*
> *that saved a wretch like me!*
> *I once was lost, but now am found; was blind but now I see.*

Still holding Mother's wrist, Doctor Stevens joined his friend in song. Their voices blended. Their breathing kept rhythm with the melody. Nora Ann nestled closer to Mother. Pamela's head rested on the bed. The men's voices filled the cabin. Alone at the end of the bed, tears streamed from Betty's eyes. Pamela put her hands to her head and her body began to shake.

Josephine was lulled by the singing. Her head began to beat with new words, "Breathing, breathing, breathing. Please Mother, please, please. Breathing, breathing, I love my mother's breathing." Then with no more than a shift of breath, Josephine felt her mother leave this world as the men sang:

Yet, when this heart and flesh shall fail,
and mortal life shall cease,
I shall possess, within the veil, a life of joy and peace.

A veil came down, and Mother was gone. "NO!" Josephine wailed. Betty and Pamela cried softly. Nora Ann startled and shrieked, "Momma! Momma!"

Mother had joined Daddy. They were four orphan girls. Their mother had waited until Reverend Miller and Doctor Stevens arrived, so they would not be alone when she died.

The four Duke sisters held on to each other for strength. Josephine remembered her father's words, "Iron is the most common element. It is in our blood and gives us strength. It can be bent by fire, but never broken—just like love."

Chapter 2: Unanswered Questions

Warren County North Carolina
Spring 1918

Four heart-broken girls looked at their mother's lifeless body through eyes filled with tears. Reverend Miller and Doctor Stevens wrapped Mother's body in her bed sheets. Then they brought in the trunk from the wagon. Doctor Stevens opened the trunk, removed a clean mattress, new bedding, and a pillow. Reverend Miller asked the girls to join him by the fire. "Doctor Stevens needs to do his work."

Josephine refused to move. She watched as Doctor Stevens carefully moved Mother's sheet-shrouded body to the floor. He then placed her old mattress in the trunk with her pillow, placing her body on the mattress. He closed the lid of the trunk.

"I hate to do this," Doctor Stevens explained, "but we need to protect you from the tuberculosis germs." Josephine's eyes locked on Doctor Stevens, and then her gaze shifted to the closed trunk. She was frozen between rage and grief. When Doctor Stevens attempted to touch her, she jerked her shoulder away and put her hand on the trunk.

Reverend Miller broke the stalemate as he approached. "Josephine, your sisters need you. Please join them by the fire." He and Doctor Stevens lifted the trunk, Betty held open the door, and Mother's body was placed in the back of the rickety wagon.

When they returned to the cabin, Doctor Stevens' eyes were filled with tears. He looked at the four Duke girls standing by the fire. He picked up his expensive leather bag, and then set it down. He hugged each of the sisters—even Josephine responded to his tears and hugged him back. His brown eyes stayed with Josephine's gaze after her hug. "We are still working on a cure." Then he wiped his eyes, straightened his shoulders, shook Reverend Miller's hand, and quietly closed the door as he left.

Nora Ann screamed when she heard the wagon leaving. "Momma, Momma."

Reverend Miller picked her up. "Don't cry Nora Ann, you have your sisters. Your mother and father are in heaven. They are covered with light and joy."

Nora Ann stopped for a moment, stiffened in his arms, and screamed louder, "Momma!"

"Where is he taking Mother's body?" Josephine asked.

"Doctor Stevens will bring your mother's body to town. He will conduct tests, prepare lab work, and make notes to discuss with fellow researchers at his Asheville clinic. I hope that one of your mother's last gifts will be to help find a cure for tuberculosis." Reverend Miller saw anger creeping into Josephine's face. "Doctor and Mrs Stevens will bring your mother's body to the church in a simple pine coffin. It won't take long."

Josephine remembered her father's simple pine coffin three years earlier. She went from mad to sad in a minute and began to cry. Pamela took her hand and they joined Betty and Nora Ann by the fire. The four girls were collapsing with grief as they huddled together. Reverend Miller sat in silence.

The sun was setting, and the room filled with shadows and sighs. Reverend Miller stood up and motioned the sisters toward the table. He served them milk with biscuits and strawberry jam. "You know how much your mother loved you. She knew that the church would protect you and not leave you alone." He was silent as they ate.

"A very good friend of mine is coming to stay with you for the next month. Her name is Mary Coffee, and I will bring her here first thing in the morning. You will only be alone for one night."

Betty answered, "Certainly, Reverend Miller, we will be fine for a night."

Nora Ann began to nod. Pamela left her chair, picked her up and moved to the rocking chair. Josephine, Betty and Reverend Miller took the new mattress and bedding and made Mother's bed. Nora Ann sighed as Pamela laid her on the bed and snuggled beside her. Her eyes fluttered as Pamela stroked her hair. Pamela could not stop her own tears and was glad Nora Ann's eyes were closed.

Josephine, Betty and Reverend Miller moved toward the fire. They pulled up chairs from the table and sat in silence. Josephine was surprised when Betty blurted out, "How are we going to pay for a funeral? Who will help us sell the farm? We are so poor."

Reverend Miller's next words enraged Josephine. Without hesitating, he responded, "Our faith promises that God will provide." Reverend Miller looked at Josephine's furious face and got a faraway look in his eyes. He closed his eyes and almost whispered, "Trouble is, God decides what He will provide."

Then Reverend Miller lost his words. Josephine understood it was hard to be a man of God when so many questions could not be answered. Life was not fair and even God could not explain why. They again sat in silence and tears.

Finally, Reverend Miller shook his head, put on his preacher face and found his words. "Betty, Doctor Stevens is my best friend. He and his wife Sarah think you are four very brave girls, and they want to help you. Sarah has a brother who is a lawyer who will work to settle your family debts with the sale of the farm. He will make sure your older stepbrothers understand the transactions. There is no money or property for anyone to inherit. He is doing this because his sister asked for help. He would never accept money from family or a friend. Doctor and Mrs Stevens will pay for the funeral."

Betty nodded. "We are grateful for their help. I have hardly slept at all wondering what we would do."

Josephine went over to the bed and lay down beside Pamela and Nora Ann. Reverend Miller smiled. "I think it is time for you girls to get some rest. I will bring in more firewood and stoke the fire. Get some sleep. I'll be back tomorrow with Miss Coffee. Say your prayers. You are in my prayers and those of all our church."

When they were alone, Betty got their nightgowns and a basin of warm water. They let Nora Ann sleep as they washed and got undressed. "Let's all sleep in Mother's bed," said Pamela. Betty and Pamela put Nora Ann and Josephine in the middle, tucked the sheets in at the sides, and snuggled down on either side of them. The bed clothes smelled new, but they were soft. Their cat, Lazy, found a spot at the bottom of the bed. Pamela closed her eyes and began to rub the edge of the blanket like she did when she was little.

Josephine did not know when she fell asleep, but it was dark when she awoke snuggled with her sisters. She crept from the bed and added wood to the fire. For a moment she caught herself listening for her mother's breathing. Tears gathered in her eyes. She wondered why Reverend Miller's friend, Miss Coffee, wanted to come and stay with them. Nothing made sense. She thought morning would never come.

Chapter 3: Dulcimer Comfort

Warren County North Carolina
Spring 1918

Betty was up early and began the day fussing. "We must make a good first impression on Miss Coffee. Here are your clean clothes." The more Betty barked orders, the slower Josephine and Pamela moved.

Betty was buttoning Nora Ann's dress, while Pamela and Josephine looked for their socks. Betty froze at the sound of the wagon coming up the lane. "Hurry up! What will Reverend Miller and Miss Coffee think if we have uncombed hair," scolded Betty. Nora Ann squirmed as Betty attempted to comb the tangles out of her hair. After Josephine put on her socks and shoes, Betty tossed her the hairbrush. Josephine ran the brush through her hair then threw it to Pamela. Pamela managed to brush her hair and pull on her shoes at the same time.

The sound of voices on the porch made the sisters stand up straight as Pamela tucked the hairbrush under a pillow. Betty called, "Come in, the door is open."

As Miss Coffee entered the cabin, Josephine again wondered why anyone would want to live in the hills with four heart-broken sisters. She studied Miss Coffee carefully. Miss Coffee was tall and slender with dark brown hair tied back in a braid fastened with an old-fashioned ivory clip. Her dress was dark blue and nicely fitted at her thin waist. The dress looked old, but not too worn. Josephine wondered if she had a hat or coat. Her shy smile and dark brown eyes calmed Josephine. Reverend Miller followed Miss Coffee, carrying her hat, coat, a worn suitcase, and an old-fashioned dulcimer. He placed the suitcase on the floor and stood beside Miss Coffee.

Betty introduced herself and shook Miss Coffee's hand. Pamela and Nora Ann did the same.

"How long will you be staying with us?" Josephine asked as she shook hands.

"I will stay for the funeral and until you find a new home."

"Why did you come to stay with us?" Josephine continued.

Reverend Miller glanced at Miss Coffee, while Betty just frowned and shook her head. Miss Coffee met Josephine's gaze and smiled. "You ask a very important question, Josephine. I think the most honest answer is that I am an orphan, too. I can understand what it feels like to lose your mother and father. My older brother, younger sister and I were orphaned when we were about your ages. I know your hearts are aching and that you don't realize you are crying, until the tears are running down your cheeks. I brought my dulcimer so we can sing. Singing always helps me when my heart is breaking."

Josephine listened and then hugged Miss Coffee. Pamela and Nora Ann did the same. Betty watched and whispered "thank you" to Reverend Miller. Betty took the hat, coat and dulcimer from him and put them on the bed behind the room divider.

Doctor Stevens had sent new sheets and blankets for Miss Coffee's bed. Reverend Miller explained, "Doctor Stevens wants us to wash up the house and make sure we air out all lingering tuberculosis danger. I hope you like washing as much as singing."

Miss Coffee smiled at Reverend Miller. "Do you like washing as much as singing?"

Reverend Miller grinned, "Girls, you can see that Miss Coffee always tells the truth—in plain English as my mother used to say. May I make us all some tea?" Betty went with Reverend Miller to fill the kettle, stoke the fire, and get the tea started.

Josephine took Miss Coffee's hand. "Miss Coffee, your bed is right behind this room divider. Our father was a good carpenter, and he made this divider so there would be some privacy in our big old open cabin. Betty hoped that we might get a doctor or nurse to sleep here and make Mother well. It never happened. I guess doctors don't like poor people…or people who live way out in the country."

Miss Coffee nodded her head and wiped a tear from her eye. "My mother and father died in our home. No doctor could be found even if we promised 'coffee'."

Josephine smiled at the coffee humor. "Our Daddy loved working with his hands. He sang mountain songs when he made the room divider. Mother said Daddy could always 'make something out of nothing.' He had some nice oak from an abandoned barn. With a little sandpaper and oil, he made the wood new again. Oh, and watch out for our cat Lazy. She thinks this is her place. She loves sleeping on the bed."

Miss Coffee put her arm around Josephine's shoulder, "You are a wonderful storyteller, Josephine. I feel like I know your Daddy already. Both my father and brother were carpenters. We are lucky to have these beautiful and useful reminders of the dear fathers and brothers we have lost."

Reverend Miller came around the room divider. "I had forgotten what a good carpenter George Duke was. I always remember him working in the fields." He put Miss Coffee's suitcase at the foot of the bed. "Well, I think I'd best be on my way." As the sisters nodded,

Reverend Miller smiled and gave Miss Coffee a little kiss on her cheek. She blushed.

Josephine's eyes narrowed, but she didn't speak. Betty showed Reverend Miller to the door and stayed on the porch until he had disappeared down the road. Miss Coffee and Josephine both noticed that Reverend Miller had not made any tea. The kettle was boiling. Josephine headed for the teapot while Pamela got the cups.

After tea, Miss Coffee asked, "What songs did your mother like?" Josephine announced that they would not be singing *Amazing Grace* ever again.

"Why is that, Josephine? It is such a lovely old hymn."

"Because it was the last song my mother ever heard on this earth and when I hear it, I remember her last breath. I don't like death in my room. It makes my heart hurt." Josephine's eyes filled with tears, and she looked down.

Miss Coffee got a faraway look in her eyes. "I don't like to remember death in a room either, Josephine. No *Amazing Grace*. Maybe we should just work for a while and talk about songs later. Working helps hearts as well as music." The morning went quickly. The girls got Miss Coffee settled and began to wash shelves and dishes as Doctor Stevens advised.

As noon approached, Miss Coffee brought out a picnic basket with sandwiches for lunch. Pamela set the table. Pamela stopped at mother's chair. "Miss Coffee, when will I stop crying as I stop at my mother's place? Why will I never set a place for her again?"

Nora Ann jumped up. "Momma and Daddy are in heaven all covered with light. When are they coming home?" The older sisters froze and looked at Miss Coffee. Miss Coffee picked up Nora Ann and sat with her in the rocking chair. She began to sing. Soon they were able to move again. The sandwiches from the church ladies were delicious, but the meal was eaten in silence.

After lunch, everyone went outside and weeded the front part of the garden where the rhubarb was growing. The sound of the robins singing soothed the ears of the Duke sisters, but nothing helped their hearts. Miss Coffee said that nature always helped her when she was sad. "My grandfather said that God walks in the garden. I do find peace when I am with growing things—even weeds."

As the cabin grew dark that evening, Miss Coffee went behind the divider and emerged with her dulcimer—followed by Lazy who had been sleeping on the bed. Miss Coffee asked, "What songs did your Mother sing?"

Josephine remembered singing *The Old Rugged Cross*. Pamela followed with *I Come to the Garden Alone*. Miss Coffee listened, as she tuned her dulcimer. "Let's sing these songs before we get ready for bed." The girls remembered more of their Mother's favorite hymns. They sang until past bedtime.

When Miss Coffee finally put down her dulcimer, they sat by the fire, lost in their thoughts and tears. It was the first time Josephine ever met someone by singing. Yet at the end of their first day together, Josephine knew Miss Mary Coffee would be her friend forever. She imagined her sisters felt the same, and loved the music still hanging in the air.

Betty broke the spell when she asked, "Miss Coffee, we won't have our farm for long. And we don't have any money either. What will happen to us?"

Miss Coffee looked serious as she spoke directly to Betty, "Sarah Stevens has ideas and money to share. But right now, I like singing more than talking about money right before bed. If you get ready, I will sing you to sleep." Betty's eyes shone with gratitude. She was the first one in her nightgown.

When all four sisters were snuggled together in their mother's bed, Josephine asked, "What about singing *The House Carpenter*? It was one of my mother and daddy's favorites."

Miss Coffee moved the rocking chair near the bed and sang:

Well met, well met, my old true love. Well met, well met, cried he.
I'm just returning from the salt, salt sea.
It's all for the love of thee.

***

For the rest of the week, the Duke girls worked with Miss Coffee on songs for their mother's funeral as they cleaned and worked in the garden. Miss Coffee told them that Doctor Stevens' wife, Sarah Stevens, would be coming early with Reverend Miller the day before the Saturday funeral. Reverend Miller would do the sermon, the children's choir would be directed by Miss Coffee, and mother would be buried next to their father in the Zion Cemetery.

Josephine remembered how Doctor Stevens' brown eyes filled with tears on the day her mother died. She wondered if Doctor and Mrs Stevens had ever lost parents or someone they loved because of tuberculosis. She wondered how it felt to be rich. She knew that Reverend Miller and Doctor Stevens were good friends, and that Miss Coffee loved Mrs Stevens like a sister.

When Josephine asked Betty her questions, Betty lost patience and reprimanded her. "You need to just listen and not ask so many questions. Sometimes your direct approach just seems rude. Will you please try?"

***

On Friday, Reverend Miller arrived in the Reilly's rickety wagon pulled by the decrepit mare. Sarah Stevens was seated beside him. As soon as the mare halted, Mrs Stevens jumped down from the wagon seat, and ran to hug Miss Coffee.

Sarah Stevens was the exact opposite of Miss Coffee. Mrs Stevens was short and curvy, in a nice ladylike way. She had blond curly hair and huge blue eyes. Like Doctor Stevens, her clothes looked rich—a long brown skirt and fitted beige jacket that had fancy braided threads all around the edges of the sleeves and collar. The buttons looked like real silver and her brown leather boots were all shined and new. She wore a little straw hat that covered most of her hair, but little golden curls kept escaping and covering her ears and hitting her pretty pink cheeks. The hat had a feather tucked in its blue silk hatband. Pamela could not take her eyes off the beautiful clothes.

Mrs Stevens looked up at the girls on the porch. Miss Coffee kept her arm around Mrs Stevens' waist as the two women walked to greet the girls. Next to Mrs Stevens, Miss Coffee suddenly looked very tall and plain. Miss Coffee introduced the sisters to Mrs Stevens from oldest to youngest.

"Sarah, this is Betty. She is the oldest sister, just like you and me." Betty smiled and Mrs Stevens gave her a hug.

"Pamela is thirteen years old and understands how to comfort her youngest sister, Nora Ann." Pamela looked very shy when she smiled at Mrs Stevens, who hesitated for a moment before giving her a hug.

"Josephine is ten years old and a good storyteller. She brings firewood each day." Josephine gestured toward the firewood pile on the porch and made a little bow. Mrs Stevens laughed.

"Nora Ann is four and loves her sisters." Nora Ann held Pamela's hand, and as Mrs Stevens approached, moved behind her sister. Mrs Stevens waved at Nora Ann as she peeked out from Pamela's side.

Mrs Stevens looked at the sisters, "I feel like I know you from all that my husband, Reverend Miller, and Miss Coffee have told me. You are very brave girls. Your mother and father would be so proud."

Reverend Miller joined them, carrying a big box. "Let's go inside, start some tea water, and see what's inside this box." The box had fancy gold lettering, "Biltmore Fine Apparel: Men's and Women's."

Betty put the kettle on the fire, while Miss Coffee offered Mrs Stevens a chair. Reverend Miller put the box on Mrs Stevens' lap.

Pamela and Nora Ann could not take their eyes off the fancy box. Josephine was much more interested in Mrs Stevens than the contents of the box. Betty joined them after placing the kettle on the fire.

Mrs Stevens removed the box lid, took off a layer of lavender tissue paper, and began to take out dresses. Three of the dresses were the same but in different sizes—navy blue with dropped waist and wide white collars. The last dress was pale blue with a wide lace collar and ruffles at the hem— for Nora Ann.

Miss Coffee handed each girl her dress, and asked, "Girls, can you try them on for us to admire?" The four sisters went behind the room screen and put on the new dresses. They fit perfectly.

Josephine thought her dress felt scratchy and the white collar made her worry that if she ate and spilled, she would have a stain that would never come out.

Betty smiled when she modeled her new dress and did a little curtsy for Mrs Stevens.

Pamela twirled around—the new dress had lifted her spirits.

Josephine stood stiffly and tried to smile when she came out.

Nora Ann followed, but still needed some help. Mrs Stevens happily tied the fancy waist ribbon and straightened her lace collar. Nora Ann looked like a little princess all in ruffles and lace. She held Mrs Stevens' hand and twirled around like Pamela.

Mrs Stevens did not think Nora Ann should go to the funeral the next day. It was during her nap time, and Mrs Stevens worried that she was too little to understand what was happening. She offered to stay with Nora Ann and come to the church after the funeral and burial.

Josephine thought no one really understood what was happening. It didn't seem fair that any of them had to attend a funeral.

Every night since Mother had died, when Nora Ann and Josephine slept in the middle of the bed, they would hold each other tight.

Whenever they heard a noise near the sink or stove, Nora Ann would say "Momma?"

Josephine had to say, "No, Nora Ann, our mother has died." Then Nora Ann would snuggle closer and whisper, "I want my Momma back home." Josephine would then hum *Swing low, Sweet Chariot*, until Nora Ann fell asleep.

***

There were lots of people at their Mother's funeral—but no relatives. As far as Josephine knew, they did not have one living relative except her stepbrothers who were grown and lived in other states.

Josephine remembered asking her father why she didn't have a grandmother. He pulled her on to his lap, "Well, my little lady, no one in our family lives long enough to meet their grandchildren. We seem to die young. I can't think of one aunt or uncle or even cousin that I could call if we needed help." Josephine realized that her children would not have grandparents either.

Betty stood by Reverend Miller and greeted people as they arrived at the church. The Reilly family rode up in their old wagon with the slow mare. They were followed by the Jackson family riding in two carriages with strong mares. The Jackson family spanned three generations. They had bought the Duke farm. The Raymond family came on foot. Josephine and Pamela walked down to meet them. "Thank you so much for the food you have sent us. Your garden is the pride of the mountain."

Most of the folks from the church were the parents of the children in the choir. A small group of women, mostly widows, had been in Mother's Bible Study group. Josephine was glad that Mrs Stevens had stayed home with Nora Ann. She could imagine Nora Ann asking the Raymond children if they had seen her mother.

When everyone was gathered in the church, Reverend Miller led the girls to the front pew. He patted Betty's shoulder as she took the seat on the aisle at the end of the pew. He went to the pulpit. Miss Coffee sat in the front with the children's choir.

When Doctor Stevens realized that the girls were sitting alone, he moved and sat next to Josephine on the other end of the pew. Josephine held Pamela's hand. Betty sat stiffly, turned her head, and smiled at Doctor Stevens.

The children's choir, under Miss Coffee's direction, sang *I Go to the Garden Alone*. Josephine couldn't sing. Just the sound of Doctor Stevens rich voice as it combined with the men in the pew behind them reminded her of when he and Reverend Miller sang *Amazing Grace* by Mother's bedside. It reminded her of the moment of her mother's last breath.

The hymn ended and the children sat down. Josephine sat with her head bowed, but not in prayer. Reverend Miller read the scripture and said a prayer. Then he left the pulpit and stood by Mother's simple pine coffin and began his eulogy.

"Mrs Duke, Patti to her friends, lived a life of faith, and one of joy. She loved her daughters, and her husband, George. After George's death, Patti Duke said that she knew we would all be joined as one in the fullness of time. She never wanted to leave her beautiful girls. 'Life is full of mystery', she would say.

"You could pray and cry at the same time with Patti Duke. It was easy to be yourself with this loving woman. Patti Duke lives in the gentleness of her daughter Betty, the singing of Pamela, the storytelling of Josephine, and Nora Ann's hugs and giggles. I always felt like I knew George Duke because of all the tales Patti shared of her beloved husband. The Duke family knew how to love. Patti Duke had faith that God would always take good care of her girls."

As Reverend Miller ended his eulogy, he looked at Betty who shook her head 'no." Not one sister could stand up and talk about their mother. Josephine kept her head down and was unable to sing.

At the end of the last prayer, the girls looked at the simple pine box. They watched as the strong men in the church lifted the coffin and took it outside to the cemetery.

Reverend Miller and Doctor Stevens led the girls out of the church, and the congregation followed. The last to arrive at the gravesite were Miss Coffee and the children's choir.

Josephine shuddered as she looked at the big opening in the earth. Doctor Stevens stood behind the girls. Then the children's choir sang the last song.

Josephine was surprised because it was not one, they had selected:

I looked over Jordan and what did I see?
Comin' for to carry me home
There was a band of angels, a-comin after me,
Comin' for to carry me home

Swing low, sweet chariot, Comin' for to carry me home
Swing low, sweet chariot, Comin' for to carry me home

I'm sometimes up, and I'm sometimes down,
Comin' for to carry me home
But I know my soul is heavenly bound,
Comin' for to carry me home

As the girls watched, Reverend Miller tossed earth on the coffin. "In the sweat of thy face shalt thou eat bread, till thou return unto the ground; for out of it wast thou taken: for dust thou art, and unto dust shalt thou return."

Josephine's mind raged. "Our Mother is not dust—and she never was!"

Chapter 4: If Truth Be Told

Warren County North Carolina
Summer 1918

After the funeral, Miss Coffee continued to live with the girls. The Stevenses left to make final arrangements for the sale of the Duke farm to the Jackson family. Reverend Miller said he would visit every Wednesday and Friday, "You can mark your calendars. I will be here rain or shine."

Each Wednesday and Friday, the girls and Miss Coffee prepared for Reverend Miller's visit. They listened for the sound of the Reilly's borrowed mare clomping up the path and would all run out to greet him. He brought food from the church ladies when he came. He greeted Miss Coffee with a big hug.

Josephine's job was to take the basket of food into the cabin. Betty would put the kettle over the fire and make tea. Reverend Miller's visit always began with a long-awaited noonday meal.

After lunch, Reverend Miller and Miss Coffee sat at the table and talked. They held hands. Josephine loved to watch Miss Coffee's eyes and smile as Reverend Miller told her about the church and asked her questions about her future classes at college.

Betty moved her sisters to the rug in front of the fire—to give Reverend Miller and Miss Coffee some "much needed privacy." The girls had just settled near the fire when Pamela announced it was "clearly love with Miss Coffee and Reverend Miller."

Josephine smiled, "I can just hear Mother and Daddy. Mother would say, 'They certainly are very fond of each other.' Daddy would have looked at us and made a kissing face." Betty and Pamela laughed as Nora Ann made a kissing face. For a moment, they felt their parents near. Home would always be where Mother and Father talked, worked and laughed.

All "love talk" ended when Miss Coffee announced that it was time to show Reverend Miller the garden, do a little more weeding and harvesting, and make some plans for dinner. The garden work lasted most of the afternoon. The garden was looking less overgrown. Betty picked the rhubarb. "Something is better than nothing," she whispered to Josephine.

***

Betty, Pamela and Josephine were very interested in Miss Coffee's life in the orphanage. As Josephine explained, "Now that we are orphans, we need to know the truth about what happens when you have no mother or father to stand up for you. What happens in a place full of children who have no parents?"

Miss Coffee told the truth and explained as only another orphan could: "The Appalachian Jackson Orphanage is about a day's ride from here, still in North Carolina. On the way you pass farms and some timberland. You can spot it because of the chapel, the rolling lawn and the construction of new student cottages.

"I was one of the first students to live in a new girls' cottage. A cottage housed twelve. Girls and boys lived in separate cottages. I lived there from the time I was twelve until I was eighteen—just two years ago. I am an old lady of twenty—just five years older than Betty. My dream is to be a teacher. I am in my second year at the Appalachian Teacher Training School.

"Doctor Wesler, the Superintendent, told me there is no finer job than teaching. I love and respect Doctor Wesler."

Nora Ann was asleep on the story rug by the fire. "But what is it really like? It can't be like home," pressed Pamela.

"Well, the most important thing was I got to stay with my little sister and older brother. My younger sister, Jean, was seven and my brother, James, was fourteen when our mother and father died of influenza. We lost our farm, the only home we had ever known, like you have. At the orphanage we lived in small cottages, ate simple food and worked hard. It was a lot like life on the farm, except for all the schoolwork.

"My music teacher, Mrs Greer, inspired me every day. She taught me to sing, play piano, and the dulcimer."

Josephine was glad that Miss Coffee understood how important it was for family to stay together. She never questioned that they all slept in the same bed. She didn't think that she and Nora Ann would ever sleep if they didn't have Miss Coffee's dulcimer and songs before bed. Miss Coffee remembered—and never sang *Amazing Grace*.

***

Josephine anticipated Reverend Miller's visits and tried to follow Betty's advice to not ask questions or seem rude. After a month of gardening and watching the "sweet talk" between Miss Coffee and Reverend Miller, Josephine decided it was time to ask the unspoken question shared by all her sisters. A man of God could be counted on to tell the truth. Josephine chose her birthday to ask her question. It was June 13 on a Wednesday and she had just turned ten.

"Reverend Miller, what is going to happen to us?" Josephine asked after dinner that night. She felt her hands clench as she spoke.

Betty was sitting in the rocking chair by the fire with Nora Ann on her lap. Miss Coffee and Pamela had moved their chairs to be by Betty at the fire. Josephine stood in front of Reverend Miller whose chair still was at the table.

"Well, Josephine, I don't know. We must trust in the Lord." Josephine looked at Miss Coffee for support. She was surprised when Miss Coffee looked away. Josephine knew that Reverend Miller was using his preacher speech to hide something. Josephine waited for an answer, but there was none.

Pamela and Betty did not look up or seem to notice that Reverend Miller had not answered the question. Josephine felt her hands tighten into fists. She was going to get an answer to the question. Miss Coffee's expression told her that Reverend Miller was not telling them something that had been decided.

Betty rocked Nora Ann while she attempted to read Mother's Bible. Nora Ann's head rested on a pillow on the chair's armrest. Betty lifted the "good book" high with one hand, while she kept her knees up by bracing them on the front rung of the chair. She needed to make sure the sleeping Nora Ann didn't roll off her lap. Josephine could not imagine anything more uncomfortable, but Betty always "made do." Josephine smiled and thought that Betty was like Daddy. She would always make do with what she had. She was also like Mother, finding comfort in the Bible.

Reverend Miller moved toward the fire to see what part of the Bible Betty was reading. Betty gave the book to Reverend Miller and lifted Nora Ann in her arms. She returned to the rocking chair after putting Nora Ann in bed. Reverend Miller stayed by the fire. Josephine brought her chair to the join her sisters and continued to stare at Reverend Miller with clenched fists.

Pamela broke the silence. "Miss Coffee, tell us more about the Appalachian Jackson Orphanage and your little sister and brother." Josephine unclenched her fists and listened. She liked hearing Miss Coffee's stories. Miss Coffee looked at Reverend Miller with a funny expression, smiled at Pamela, and began:

"At Appalachian, we just got into a routine and worked. And I sang. I had learned to whistle when I was only four. Miss Greer used my ability to whistle and keep a tune—I was one of the youngest soloists in the school choir. She told me I had perfect pitch and it was always easy for me to learn a song—sometimes just from hearing it only once.

"My sister loved to read and would read to my older brother and me every evening after dinner—right before chapel. My brother worked in the school wood shop making things we needed for the school. He and his friends had to work mostly with scrap wood. At the orphanage, we turned everything into an advantage. The carpenter teachers took those scraps of wood and taught the boys to make lovely parquet patterns in their trays and furniture. When I graduated, I asked for a small footstool that my brother had made for our cottage. I have it with my winter clothes stored at the parsonage. I'll show it to you sometime.

"My brother died in The Great War," she continued. "He was only nineteen and died of influenza in his first year of service. He was waiting to be shipped overseas to France when he died."

Reverend Miller moved from the fire to stand behind Miss Coffee. He placed his hands on her shoulders, and she turned her head and looked up at him. The room was silent except for the crackle of the fire. Josephine's thoughts turned to Mother and Miss Coffee's brother—death hovered in the room. Like wood, memories stoked their fires of grief.

"In the orphanage, we eventually stopped thinking about what we had lost. When you are surrounded by people who have all lost their parents, and some their brothers and sisters, you realize that everyone is in the same boat. If you forbid me to sing *Amazing Grace*, Josephine, I forbid you to sing *Row, row, row your boat*. We were not going merrily down the stream."

Josephine nodded as Miss Coffee whispered, "As you row, there are always empty seats for those you lost."

Miss Coffee stood up, went behind the divider and returned with her dulcimer. "No more talk of songs that make us sad. I'll check on Nora Ann while you girls get ready for bed. Then we can sing before we sleep."

Reverend Miller announced it was time for him to go. Miss Coffee put down her dulcimer and went out with him to the porch.

Josephine waited until their kiss and hug ended. Then she ran out to join them. The door banged behind her. "Reverend Miller, I am tired of worrying about the Reilly's mare falling down the mountain and taking you with her. Get yourself a new horse. I don't trust that old nag—the worst excuse for a horse in Warren County as my Daddy would have said." Josephine stood with her feet spread and her hands on her hips. She needed everyone to know she was serious.

Reverend Miller stood with his arm around Miss Coffee and shook his head. "Well, Miss Josephine, I hope they have some nice free horses hanging on trees along this path. That's the only way I could get a horse, but I will do my best. See you on Friday."

"Good and remember you did not answer my question about what will happen to us. Your answer will help me trust in the Lord."

Miss Coffee looked down, and Reverend Miller stopped smiling. Josephine was relentless. Reverend Miller bent over to look at Josephine face to face. "I'll be ready."

***

Miss Coffee's singing eased their sadness, and her stories about her family and the Appalachian Jackson Orphanage made them feel less alone.

They spent hours in the garden and tried as best they could to make the yard and gardens better for the Jackson family. They continued to follow Doctor Stevens' advice and washed dishes and surfaces before the Jackson's moved in with their family and young grandchildren.

On Friday, Josephine insisted that they all wait on the porch for Reverend Miller. "Today Reverend Miller promised to tell us what will happen to us. It will be my belated birthday present."

Miss Coffee told Betty and Pamela about Josephine's warning to Reverend Miller to "not worry us by riding the worst excuse for a horse in Warren County." Betty was just about to lecture Josephine on her manners, when they saw Reverend Miller riding up the path.

Josephine shouted, "Where did he get that horse?!"

Reverend Miller was riding a brand-new horse with a shining bridle, and fancy hand-tooled leather saddle. As he approached the porch, he slowed and reined the horse to a halt. Josephine ran down the steps. "Reverend Miller, are horses hanging on trees these days?"

"Well, Miss Josephine, just let me get off this fine young colt and I'll tell you." He dismounted, tied the reins to the porch railing, walked up the steps to the porch, and gave Miss Coffee a hug. He turned to Josephine, "When I told Sarah Stevens that I had promised you I would not be using the Reilly's fine old, crippled mare and that I thought I would be walking, she was very interested. She told me to come back the next morning, and that she would have a big surprise."

"She bought you a horse?" shouted Pamela. Miss Coffee and Betty just shook their heads in disbelief.

Josephine laughed. "Well, I guess wishes can become horses for poor folks to ride."

Reverend Miller gave a slight bow to Josephine. "I couldn't believe my eyes when her carriage man brought this thoroughbred mare out of their barn. Sarah said that you were right, Josephine. I must always be able to arrive as soon as my flock needed me. She said she believed in all the people she had met after your mother's funeral and during her stay with you. She and Doctor Stevens want to make sure your neighbors have their pastor arriving as soon as he is needed. Her name is Trotter."

"It must be nice to have all that money to give such big presents," Josephine returned.

"Well, Josephine, I don't have any better friends than Matt and Sarah Stevens."

Then he looked at Miss Coffee and smiled. "Well, except for Miss Coffee." She smiled back and did not blush this time. "When your friends offer you a gift that lets you serve the people you love, you take the gift. Or at least, I did."

Josephine looked at Reverend Miller. "Mother told us to never look a gift horse in the mouth. Daddy said if something looked too good to be true, it probably was. He thought it was a good idea to look in the horse's mouth."

"Reverend Miller, don't you think it is funny that Trotter is a gift horse? I think we should look in his mouth to make my daddy happy."

Reverend Miller and Miss Coffee looked at Josephine and burst into laughter. "Well, his molars are yours for an inspection, Miss Josephine. As for me, I am mighty hungry after my ride up the mountain."

Suddenly, Josephine's stomach growled. "You're right, Reverend Miller. I'm better off putting something in my mouth than looking in some horse's mouth. I smell those biscuits, Miss Coffee. Can I help you set the table for lunch?"

Betty watered Trotter, while Pamela lifted Nora Ann so she could pet her back. Trotter stood still and wasn't bothered by all the attention from strangers. When they finished and came inside, Miss Coffee was just taking biscuits off the skillet. They washed their hands while Josephine and Miss Coffee served the meal.

The table was laden with biscuits, fried chicken leftovers from Reverend Miller's church luncheon, rhubarb that Miss Coffee had cooked with wild strawberries Josephine had picked near the robin's nest, and milk from the Jackson family. They ate and laughed. Josephine reminded herself to wait until after the meal to ask for answers.

***

After lunch, Reverend Miller said he had some serious business to discuss. Josephine was suspicious when he switched to his minister voice. "Miss Coffee has been telling you about her life at the Appalachian Jackson Orphanage. Doctor Wesler, the superintendent of the orphanage, is a dedicated educator and only hires the finest staff and teachers. They just built a new library and swimming pool. New cottages are being built to meet the needs of the growing number of orphans in

North Carolina. Tuberculosis and influenza have become a plague claiming the lives of hundreds of adults and leaving thousands of children orphans. Doctor Wesler and the Orphanage Board receive letters from churches all over Appalachia each week."

"Excuse me, Reverend Miller," Josephine interrupted. "Are you telling us that we are going to live at the orphanage? That we will all be together, and live in a cottage like Miss Coffee and her sister and brother?"

Betty gave Josephine a "watch yourself, don't interrupt and speak only when you are spoken to" look. Josephine ignored Betty and turned to Miss Coffee. She was upset when Miss Coffee's eyes fell to the folded hands in her lap. Why did Miss Coffee look away every time Josephine asked her question about the future?

Reverend Miller's voice softened, "Josephine, you are right that I am talking about a move to the Appalachian Jackson Orphanage, but I am not talking about all of you going together."

"Wha-attt?" stuttered Josephine. "Miss Coffee told us that North Carolina churches believed in keeping families together. Remember, the Lord is watching you, Reverend Miller."

Reverend Miller caught Miss Coffee's eye. Miss Coffee had a funny expression for a tiny second—an "I told you so" expression, that was gone in an instant.

Reverend Miller had changed back to his serious minister's voice. Betty moved over and stood behind Josephine. She placed her hands on her sister's shoulders and looked like she was prepared to strangle Josephine to keep her quiet.

Josephine kept silent as Reverend Miller dropped his bombshell.

"You girls know how much Doctor and Mrs Stevens think of you. What you may not know is that they have wanted to have a family of their own for years, but God has not blessed them with children. Let me read the Stevenses' letter so you can hear their proposal in their own words."

The letter began with Mrs Stevens telling the Duke sisters how much she and Doctor Stevens wanted a family. They had a warm and loving home and would be wonderful parents. They wondered if they could visit and talk about this. They would like Nora Ann and Josephine to come and live with them and be their family.

"How could they love us and not want to take all four of us to live with them? Look how scrawny we are. We don't eat much, and we are good at sharing beds," Josephine demanded as she felt Betty's hands tightening on her shoulders.

Miss Coffee looked up and met Josephine's eyes with what looked like sympathy. But when she looked at Reverend Miller, her eyes returned to her lap.

Reverend Miller continued. "Josephine, all I am asking is for you to talk to Doctor and Mrs Stevens. They will be coming up the mountain in an hour so we can talk about this together. Nothing has been decided. But you must promise to listen to what they have to say."

This was a trap. Josephine could feel it. It wasn't just Betty's hands squeezing her shoulders; it was the very air in the room—the air that smelled of adults who have already decided and are pretending that you have a choice.

Miss Coffee got up, avoided Josephine's eyes, and said that she would clear up the lunch dishes. Then she asked the girls to change into the pretty dresses Mrs Stevens had given them for the funeral. Betty and Pamela put on the navy and white dresses and laid out Nora Ann's so they could change her when she awoke from her nap.

Josephine did not change her dress. She sat near the fire with her arms crossed over her chest. She refused to talk to anyone.

Josephine remembered the smells of the cabin when Mother cooked, her Daddy's laughter, the feel of the old wooden spoon that Mother used to stir her soups, and the day they found Lazy their cat. She thought of the bed that she and Nora Ann shared with their sisters and of the view of the mountains that greeted them each morning. Her mind seethed. We are losing all of this and now they want to separate us? A voice inside her head calmed her: "Stay where you are. Don't move for anybody! The foes are about to arrive. At the end of the day, the poor Duke sisters must be together. No rich folks can separate us."

Chapter 5: Friend or Foe

Defense Heights Maryland
August 1958

I loved when my parents quoted famous people. My mother Josephine did it more often than my father. She had been schooled in the fine art of memorization. She loved to quote Lincoln: "Come what will, I will keep my faith with friend and foe."

I never thought to ask my mother about her foes. I felt like I knew all her friends very well. She told stories about their adventures, and we visited them in Washington DC and Maryland. Mother encouraged me to develop friendships. Many of my best friends were the daughters of her friends. But even my mother's closest friends did not know she was an orphan.

One day when I was pestering my mother about her life as an orphan, she revealed one of the foes of her childhood—a ghost from her past. This ghost was a rich person from Asheville, North Carolina, who attempted to separate Josephine and her sisters. Her face became hard as she told her story.

"Nora Ann and I were sent to live with some rich people in Asheville. I had to pitch a fit until they let us join our big sisters in the orphanage. As an adult, I realized that our lives might have been different growing up with a rich and educated family in Asheville. As a child, I had only one thought. I must be with my sisters."

Even at the age of twelve, I understood the truth in my mother's words. Families must never be torn asunder. Iron is in our blood for a reason and our foes will be vanquished.

Warren County North Carolina
August 1918

Josephine did not get up when the Stevenses arrived an hour later in their own carriage with a driver and two horses. It was like Cinderella.

Nora Ann was just waking when they came in the door. Mrs Stevens immediately went and hugged her. She dressed Nora Ann in the pale blue dress with the lacy collar. It only took Doctor and Mrs Stevens a few minutes to tell the girls what Reverend Miller had already said. They wanted Nora Ann and Josephine to live with them for six months to see if they could be their new family.

Josephine scowled and cleared her throat to speak—to demand that the four sisters stay together.

Before Josephine could say a word, Betty stood up. "Doctor and Mrs Stevens, I want to speak for Pamela and myself. I thank you for your wonderful offer. Pamela and I feel that we have had many years with a loving mother and father. We are grateful for the religious and educational opportunities at the Appalachian Jackson Orphanage."

Pamela looked at her lap, while Betty continued. "We believe our younger sisters would benefit from having more years with a mother and father. Your home sounds lovely, and I know that Josephine and Nora Ann would be wonderful daughters."

Josephine's eyes flashed and her mind raged. Pamela and Miss Coffee sat and looked at their hands folded in their laps. Josephine scowled thinking that laps are very interesting, especially when you are selling your own flesh and blood down the river.

For the first time, her fury kept her from speaking. All eyes in the room were on her. Silence gathered in the air and rained down on all those hands folded in laps, and on the patient faces of Mr and Mrs Stevens.

Finally, Miss Coffee stood up. "Josephine, would you please step outside with me for a minute?"

Josephine stood up, stomped toward the door, and stormed out, banging it with a loud crack. Miss Coffee followed as everyone in the cabin watched in silence. They stepped off the porch and began to walk the path toward the newly tended garden.

When they reached the garden, Miss Coffee spoke. "Josephine, I want you to know how brave I think you are. You are a wonderful sister. I don't think Nora Ann would be able to smile or sleep if you weren't with her. But school is starting in the fall, and we all need to think about the future. Your farm will be sold in the next weeks. I have told you all about Appalachian, but I think it very important for you to find out about Asheville. Mrs Stevens and I have been writing letters, so I could answer her questions, and tell her all about you. You know the Stevenses have a beautiful big house and have wanted children for many years. I think you and Nora Ann should just go for a little visit. You will need to stay long enough to see the schools and make friends. Nora Ann will stay at home with Mrs Stevens. Mrs Stevens is so excited to show you the room she has prepared for you and Nora Ann. She has bought some lovely new clothes." Miss Coffee stopped.

Josephine snapped, "I thought you were my friend. I thought you understood about family. I thought you knew that clothes don't make a person special. Old dresses are just fine if you know the sisters that wore them first."

Miss Coffee's eyes pleaded, "I do understand! Reverend Miller and I have talked endlessly about this. You can ask any questions you want. But you already know—you don't have a choice. You have to give this a try."

"It is very clear that I don't have a choice, and that Nora Ann is too trusting to know what is going on!" The thought of losing Betty and Pamela right after Mother's death made her so mad, she could hardly breathe.

Then in a heartbeat, her mind opened. She had a foe, and she had a plan. This was a foe she could defeat, and she knew how. She went from fury to ice. She knew how she would reunite the sisters. She would wear her Iron Pants and bide her time.

Miss Coffee reached for Josephine's hand, and froze before their hands touched. Josephine transformed before her eyes and her expression went from murderous to calm. A strong, new Josephine spoke, "We can go back to the cabin. I will be polite and give this change a try. Promise me that you will visit both Asheville and Appalachian, and that we only have to try this for six months. Promise!"

"I promise, Josephine. I promise," she said squeezing her hand.

As they walked back to the cabin, Miss Coffee watched Josephine out of the corner of her eye. Miss Coffee could almost hear the wheels in Josephine's head turning. She felt Josephine's new strength—like iron. It was a strength they shared.

***

When they entered the cabin, they were surprised at the sound of laughter. Mrs Stevens looked at Miss Coffee saying, "These boys can't seem to get together without telling stories of their college days. Makes me glad to think that I will only be raising girls." She laughed.

Mrs Stevens had set out lemonade and homemade oatmeal raisin cookies on fancy little China plates. A lemon meringue pie was cut into small slices. Josephine heaped her plate with cookies and a sliver of pie. She laughed when Doctor Stevens and Reverend Miller told their stories. Miss Coffee was the only one who kept looking at Josephine with concern.

"Did I ever tell you the one about Doctor Stevens taking a New Testament class with me?" asked Reverend Miller. "I had to promise him a meal if he took the class. Matt Stevens was the only student who ever made the head of our theology department, Professor Taylor, laugh. When our 'men of the cloth' drifted into platitudes, Matt was there to break their pious spell.

"His words stay with me to this day. 'Ah, faith in action, there's the rub. Really welcoming the stranger who wants to eat your food and marry your daughter.

Your relatives are furious. Your congregation is ready to stone you. Doin' what Jesus says is gonna make them mad as Hades.' Matt was a new voice in our class, for sure.

"My favorite class began when Doctor Taylor quoted the gospel of Matthew 26:11: *For ye have the poor always with you...* and asked about the Church's duty to the poor. Some of our classmates proposed that we did not really need to worry too much about the poor. We just needed to concentrate on Jesus."

"Matt fired back, 'I am sure if Jesus were here today, he would wonder at your logic. He would certainly disagree with your conclusions. I think poor really does mean poor. Your assurances that we probably won't have to help them until the end of time are just wrong.'"

Reverend Miller looked at his friend with both love and amusement. "Matt always ended his challenging remarks with a dramatic flourish of his hand and a nod toward our professor. Doctor Taylor would roar with laughter—a laugh that immediately silenced any student under Matt's attack."

As Reverend Miller finished his story, Doctor Stevens looked at the group and gave a dramatic hand flourish while nodding toward Reverend Miller. Everyone laughed. Josephine couldn't help but like

Doctor Stevens. She remembered the tears in his eyes when he took Mother's body away.

She also remembered that sisters stay together. She could hold her ground. She was bound by love. Iron ran in her veins. Iron Pants was her new name, and the Battle of Asheville would be won.

Chapter 6: Leaving Home

Defense Heights Maryland
October 1963

My father, Cleophas, told stories. Unlike my mother, he was never a natural teller of tales. When he told a story, you had to search for the moral in his short and stark narratives:

Elaine, did I ever tell you about stealing apples with my brothers? One day, Joe, Dan and I were walking home from school. We could smell the apples on the other side of the fence before we even turned down our neighbor's lane. Joe said, "Come on! Let's get a few of those red, ripe apples. No one is watching." We climbed over the fence and began to eat apples and stuff them in our pockets.

Suddenly, we heard our neighbor yelling and we saw him running toward us. My older brothers cleared the fence in a second, but my overalls got caught. Our neighbor caught me and gave me a spanking—just like I was one of his own kids.

And my brothers, where were they? They were standing on the other side of the fence laughing. The End.

After years of reflection and watching my father with his family, I realized the lesson. Just as my father would never have abandoned his brothers, he expected brothers and sisters to stand together. He would have stayed until all the brothers were all over the fence. Cleophas Frank Piatt would never laugh at the misfortune of a brother—*Never*!

Warren County North Carolina
August 1918

Josephine treasured each day with her sisters as they prepared to leave their farm forever. Mrs Stevens sent four new steamer trunks—fine leather and brass with wooden hangers and two compartments. The inside was lined with flowered cloth. Betty worried about all the money the Stevenses were spending. "We could have gotten by with just two trunks, one for Appalachian Jackson Orphanage and one for Asheville," she lamented.

Josephine agreed. "When my trunk is packed, we will still have room for furniture, Nora Ann and the cat." Mrs Stevens said Nora Ann and Josephine could bring

Lazy, their cat, with them. The Stevenses had a cat named Daisy. Nora Ann thought it was funny that she would be able to call "Lazy Daisy," and two cats would come. Everyone loved hearing Nora Ann laugh. Josephine never knew a cat that would come when called.

When the sisters began packing, Miss Coffee told them to each take a family treasure. Mother's Bible was saved for Nora Ann because the baby deserved the most precious gift. Mother was never without her Bible. Betty took a beautiful, embroidered handkerchief. Pamela claimed Mother's favorite teacup painted with English ivy and roses. Josephine found Daddy's old red and black plaid shirt and made it into a little blanket for Nora Ann. She loved it and began to rub her cheek against it when she was going to sleep.

Josephine could not choose. She thought of taking one of her daddy's old pipes, but it was too smelly. She finally chose a spoon and Mother's hairbrush—things her mother had touched every day. As Josephine packed the spoon and hairbrush in her trunk, she hoped she would not have to hit anyone with them. Josephine had been taught by her mother not to fight or hit. She preferred to use words to win her battles—not weapons. The best way to use words were in stories. Good stories always told it like it was.

Josephine was already thinking of stories that explained why sisters could never be torn apart—even by those who wanted to love them and could afford to give them the best of everything. These stories would hurt more than a slap ever could. She began to count their remaining days together. In her heart, she hoped something would stop this train.

***

The Jackson family bought the Duke farm. Their furniture and farm tools would become the Jacksons' property. The legal work had been completed by Mrs Steven's brother, the Honorable Mark Claxton. All the taxes had been paid, and legal transfers of property signed. The stepbrothers had agreed to all the arrangements.

Mr Claxton began his work with a search for any other living Duke relatives. When he and Mrs Stevens visited one day, Josephine told him her father's stories that no one lived long enough to meet their grandchildren. After a week searching courthouse records, he confirmed that the Dukes did die young.

Josephine asked Mr Claxton how the law helped poor people. She asked why their family could not have a doctor when their parents were sick. Mr Claxton mumbled something about asking Doctor Stevens.

Doctor Stevens only shook his head when she asked him where the doctors were and why he had arrived too late to save their mother. Again, she saw tears in his eyes. The future of the four girls would be supervised by Reverend Miller and Doctor Stevens, with the oversight of the Warren County Court.

Josephine realized the coming changes were not easy for anyone, and that laws could only do so much. She would be on her own soon, with Nora Ann to protect. She would put on her Iron Pants. The train could not be stopped.

***

The day for the Duke sisters to be separated arrived. The cabin was scrubbed as clean as possible and aired out. The four trunks stood like sentinels inside the cabin door. It was hard to move around them. Each trunk contained a sister's treasures, a few clothes and shoes. As Josephine had predicted, there was room for stowaways in the sadly empty trunks.

As the Stevenses' carriage pulled up the lane, the girls stood by Miss Coffee on the cabin porch. The coachman helped Mrs Stevens out of the carriage. She would stay with Nora Ann and Josephine, until the three of them left for Asheville the next day. Mrs Stevens hugged Miss Coffee and put her arm around Betty.

Josephine watched Mrs Stevens. How would she feel as she watched the sisters say goodbye to each other? Could Miss Coffee step up and save the day?

Miss Coffee looked as sad as Josephine felt, but she did not attempt to stop anything. In her mind, Josephine understood Miss Coffee's dilemma. She loved Doctor and Mrs Stevens. She also knew the pain of family separation because of her experiences and her big heart. She was emphatic that Josephine had to try living in Asheville and that Nora Ann needed her. Josephine appreciated Miss Coffee's honesty and insights. Miss Coffee would not be surprised when Josephine put up a fight when she got to Asheville. She wondered if Miss Coffee liked a good fight as much as a good story. She was happy that she could fight with stories.

Miss Coffee asked Josephine to take Mrs Steven's overnight bag inside. Then Josephine held open the door for the Stevenses' carriage driver as he loaded Betty's and Pamela's trunks in the back of the carriage. Mrs Stevens began to talk to Betty and Pamela as they moved off the porch to make room for the carriage driver.

The carriage driver was tall and lean and gave Josephine a half smile and nod as he swung the trunks up and carefully moved them from inside the cabin, down the porch, into the carriage. He was about the same age as the oldest of the Duke stepbrothers.

Josephine wondered if he liked his job and where he'd grown up.

Doctor Stevens had purchased three train tickets for Appalachian Jackson Orphanage that Mrs Stevens gave to Miss Coffee as they watched the trunks being loaded. Betty and Pamela were comforted that Miss Coffee could stay with them at the orphanage until they got settled. Miss Coffee was looking forward to seeing some of her teachers at Appalachian Jackson and getting their advice on her college studies.

After her stay, Miss Coffee would take the train to Boone and resume her life at the Appalachian Teacher's College. She would live in a rooming house where she helped in the kitchen to pay for room and board. Her classes would begin in early September. Josephine was glad that Miss Coffee could go back to college. She would be a wonderful teacher and her dream was important to the Duke sisters, the Stevenses and Reverend Miller. Betty and Pamela were in good hands. Josephine felt even more alone as she watched the carriage man tie the trunks on the back of the carriage.

When Josephine hugged Betty goodbye, she began to cry. "I love you, Betty. You are the best big sister. You took good care of us all. You are our comfort. Mother and Daddy would be so proud of you. We will be together soon. Take care of Pamela."

Betty took out Mother's handkerchief and helped Josephine with her tears. Nora Ann hugged Betty's waist and refused to let go. Betty lifted Nora Ann into her arms as Pamela hugged Josephine. Josephine could feel Pamela's sadness seep into her own heart. "Miss Coffee and Reverend Miller will visit you. I will write," Josephine whispered. Pamela smiled when Josephine mentioned Miss Coffee, and she kissed her sister.

Miss Coffee took Pamela's hand as they walked toward the carriage. Mrs Stevens took Nora Ann in her arms as she walked to the carriage with Betty. Josephine stood alone at the bottom of the cabin steps.

Suddenly, Betty turned and ran back to Josephine. Putting her arms around her, Betty whispered, "You only have to try this, Josephine. We will always be your family. You will always know how to find us."

"I know and I love my sisters," she whispered back.

Betty walked toward the carriage, and the carriage man helped her in. They waved goodbye, as it disappeared down the lane.

As soon as the carriage left, the anger grew in Josephine's chest. She told Mrs Stevens that she was going down to the meadow to pick some strawberries. Mrs Stevens got a pretty little basket, emptied it, and handed it to the scowling Josephine. Mrs Stevens looked at Josephine to see if she and Nora Ann were invited to come and pick berries. Josephine turned on her heel without a word.

When Josephine approached the meadow, she looked back and saw Mrs Stevens rocking Nora Ann on the porch. From a distance, she looked like any mountain mother loving her child. She even hummed a mountain tune. How could she not understand?

Josephine sat on the stump of an old tree for the whole afternoon, and never looked for a strawberry. She began to think of reuniting her sisters. An idea began to form—her first story to warn Mrs Stevens what was ahead. Stories would be her weapons.

***

Mrs Stevens and Nora Ann came looking for Josephine in the late afternoon. Nora Ann took Josephine's hand and whispered, "Betty and Pamela went away in a big carriage. They are going to school. We are going to Asheville." Josephine nodded at Nora Ann. It was good that Nora Ann really didn't understand much of what was happening. They walked toward the cabin. Mrs Stevens didn't say a word. She seemed to understand that nothing she had to say would comfort Josephine.

The sadness of knowing that this was the last night they would be in their cabin was crushing Josephine. Mrs Stevens served chicken, biscuits and potato salad for dinner—with lemon meringue pie for dessert. Josephine's only words during dinner were, "I wish that Betty and Pamela could have shared this meal with us. I always thought we would leave at the same time."

The carriage driver would return in the morning. Mrs Stevens had kept Josephine's and Nora Ann's nightgowns out of their trunks. After they washed and dressed for bed, Josephine asked Mrs Stevens if she knew any stories.

"I bought some books for you and Nora Ann, but they are in your room in Asheville. Would you like to tell a story before we go to bed tonight? Miss Coffee told me what a good storyteller you are."

"Yes, I would love to tell a story, one I learned from my real mother. She told stories every night to her four girls. She wouldn't think of telling a story until we were all four together." Mrs Stevens looked so sad that Josephine almost stopped her plan. But Josephine knew that Iron Pants could tell the story. "I never begin with 'Once upon a time,'" Josephine told Mrs Stevens, "I just jump into the action. Are you ready?" Mrs Stevens nodded, rocked Nora Ann, and tried to smile. Josephine told her tale—her iron had returned.

Outsmarting Sister Rich Fox

Sister Rich Fox watched until the four Little Rabbits were all alone in their house. Sister Rich Fox wanted a nice little rabbit pie for dinner. Being a nice Southern lady fox, she knew she couldn't eat little rabbits for no reason. She had a wily plan. She would make the rabbits disobey her.

Southern animals understood the rule, "Do what the big folks tell you to do." If the Little Rabbits disobeyed Big Sister Rich Fox, they could become pie for sure!

Sister Rich Fox took a piece of sugar cane out of her bag. She walked up to the Rabbit house and pushed open the front door. The four Little Rabbits were sitting by the fire and looked up at her. "Little Rabbits, can you please break up this sugar cane for me? I need my sugar so I can stay sweet," she commanded.

Those Little Rabbits tried to break that strong stick of sugar cane. They thought they were too puny to do it.

"I am losing all my sweetness. Bring that cane to me now," howled Sister Rich Fox.

Those four Little Rabbits knew they could become a pie if they didn't do something quick. They had to obey, but they didn't think they were strong enough to break that cane.

Suddenly, they heard the song of a robin close by in a tree. They listened carefully to the words of his song: *"Take your teeth and chew that cane. Chew and gnaw, once again. See the weak spot, make it break."*

Sister Rich Fox was not pleased when the Little Rabbits broke the sugar cane and gave it to her. The Little Rabbits guessed that she would not get any sweeter after she ate it, and they were right!

In a minute, Sister Rich Fox growled. *"Little rabbits, I am so thirsty after all the sweet sugar. Please take this sifter down to the pump and bring me some water. I am dying of thirst."* Those rabbits ran to the pump, but all the water just ran through that sifter filled with holes.

Again, they heard the song of the robin: *"Take some moss and line the holes. Now take some clay and spread away. Plug the holes and drink away."* The Little Rabbits did as the robin told them. They ran up to Sister Rich Fox and bowed as they handed her the sifter full of sweet well water.

Just as she took the water, a friendly bear came up the lane. The rabbits ran down the lane to meet their friend Bear. The Bear growled when he saw Sister Rich Fox. He showed his teeth. Sister Rich Fox had to go home all alone and hungry. The End

As Josephine told her story, Mrs Stevens rocked Nora Ann, and began to get a wary look in her eyes. Mrs Stevens stopped rocking. Nora Ann was asleep.

Josephine's voice became more dramatic as she finished her tale.

Mrs Stevens looked at Josephine. "You are a wonderful storyteller—just like your mother. I want to learn more about the Little Rabbits. I am so glad we will have time to tell stories and have fun in Asheville." Then Mrs Stevens' eyes filled with tears. "You know that I am not Sister Rich Fox, don't you Josephine?"

"Yes, ma'am. I know you are a very nice rich lady who wants to have some little girls—but not to eat for dinner."

"Josephine, I will never replace your mother. I know you would like to be with your sisters. But all I want is for you to try being our family for a few months. You might be surprised that you like our house. I do not want to hurt you in any way. But I would love to have little rabbits all my own."

The carriage arrived after breakfast the next day. When their two trunks were loaded, Josephine got into the carriage with Nora Ann and Mrs Stevens. Mrs Stevens immediately put Nora Ann on her lap. Josephine held Lazy the cat.

Josephine looked out the window, and tried to memorize every tree, flower and bird as they rode down the lane for the last time. She remembered watching the dogwood tree for a sign of spring. She remembered climbing trees as her daddy watched. She remembered picking flowers from the fields for her parents. She could not remember ever thinking that she would have to leave, and never come home again.

Chapter 7: Battle of Asheville

King Ferry New York
April 2018

One of my mother's favorite sayings was: "The more things change, the more they stay the same." As a child, I thought this was a very silly idea. But as the years roll by, I see the truth in these words. I share my mother's worries about war, leaders who lack morals and ideals, and protecting and serving the poor in our midst. When I wrote about the death of my mother's parents, I wondered if health care had improved in the last hundred years.

To satisfy my curiosity, I did an internet search on health care in rural Warren County, North Carolina, in 2018. An article proclaimed Warren County a "primary care desert." The statistics were staggering:

The numbers show that Warren County only has 0.49 doctors per 10,000 residents. By comparison, in Orange County, the home of the University of North

Carolina-Chapel Hill, there are approximately 112 doctors per 10,000 residents.

Home is where the heart is, but when do you have to leave to stay well? The more things change, the more they stay the same. Where would help be found for the poor in my Mother's mountains?

Asheville North Carolina
Fall 1918

Josephine rolled over as she felt the sun on her face. She kept her eyes shut and imagined the sound of her mother singing. She could see her mother as she rattled the iron skillet to make the morning meal of grits and eggs. Nora Ann slept beside her and snuggled closer when she moved. Josephine tried to remember the sun coming through their window at home. The window frame rattled in her imagination and for a moment she could see her mountains. In her mind, the sun rose behind their peaks in colors of pinks, reds and purples.

She opened her eyes to her Asheville reality and her resolve to reunite the Duke sisters. *Red sky at morning, Doctor and Mrs Stevens take warning!* Iron Pants needed to be ready at the start of the day. Josephine found her courage.

She looked at the window in their new room. Unlike home, there was no morning-red sky mountain framed by chipped-paint wood and dusty ledges. Here a wide freshly painted pale blue sill held sparkling windowpanes encased in fancy lace curtains held back by blue velvet sashes.

Nora Ann sighed. Josephine hoped Nora Ann's dreams were as sweet as her face, with her cheeks softly lined from the pillowcase seams. Josephine sat up. No more time for sweetness. It was time to start the day and wage war. The sisters had to be reunited. The first battle of the day began when Josephine started to cry. She pretended that she had a bad dream. She thought about the Reilly's wagon and mare falling off a bridge with Betty and Pamela driving.

As soon as she started to sob, Nora Ann woke up and began crying too. Josephine knew what would happen next. Mrs Stevens came into the room. "There, there, my dear little girls. I am here. Your new mother is here." Whatever Mrs Stevens said always made Josephine cry harder. Mrs Stevens looked so sad and weary. The morning crying plan was wearing everyone down. Since the sisters had arrived, no day began without sobbing and Josephine's tales of bad dreams.

The tearful girls were a stark contrast to the bedroom lovingly decorated by Mrs Stevens. Pretty blue and white forget-me-not quilts adorned two canopy beds that sat side by side in the middle of their large sunny room. The lace curtains framed two big windows facing the backyard, with a view of the formal landscaped gardens. There was a wardrobe full of pretty dresses and shoes, and a toy box overflowing with games, dolls and puzzles. Of the two beds, only one had ever been used. Nora Ann slept with Josephine every night.

In a minute, Doctor Stevens stood in the doorway wearing a bathrobe over his trousers and shirt. He observed the morning scene—two crying girls, and an exhausted wife, herself on the verge of tears. He came into the room and slowly sat in the rocking chair near the window. Lazy followed Doctor Stevens everywhere. As soon as he sat down, Lazy jumped on his lap. Josephine remembered that Lazy was always Daddy's cat.

Mrs Stevens picked up Nora Ann, who stopped crying. She patted her back and Nora Ann went back to sleep. Josephine took a little lacy handkerchief from a box on a fancy table by the bed and blew her nose. She described her bad dream in detail, ending with her sisters in the wagon that fell down the mountain. Mrs Stevens shook her head and wiped her tears. "It was only a bad dream, Josephine. Your sisters are safe and well at Appalachian. I promise. Let's get dressed. Today is your first day of school."

When Josephine first arrived in Asheville, Doctor and Mrs Stevens spent a lot of time taking her to see the elementary school and talking about the importance of a fine education. Mrs Stevens had an uncle who was the superintendent of the schools in Asheville. After he retired, a new school was named after him. Josephine realized that the Stevenses knew everyone that had something named after them—the bank, the school, a library at the college, and the new wing of the hospital. There were buildings named after the Duke family, but these were no relatives of Josephine. She was a poor Duke, not a Biddle Duke and she better not forget it! The only Dukes she cared about were the four Duke orphan girls and how they needed to stay together.

After she returned from the school tours, Josephine began to plan for her first day of school. Now the morning had finally arrived. She wore one of her old dresses and didn't tie her hair back in the new pretty ribbons Mrs Stevens left on her dresser. She made an old-fashioned braid and tied it with a faded ribbon. Josephine came downstairs and was still wiping her eyes from her crying. Mrs Stevens didn't say anything about Josephine's appearance as she served breakfast. She chatted about all the new friends Josephine would make in school, and what a fine teacher Miss Bean was. Josephine ate her scrambled eggs, and biscuits with homemade strawberry jam. She kept her eyes down as Mrs Stevens talked.

After breakfast, Doctor Stevens walked with Josephine to the Claxton Elementary school—named after Mrs Stevens' uncle. He stayed with her as she met her teacher, Miss Bean. Josephine carried her new notebook, pen and pencil. Doctor Stevens had his own little notebook to write down other supplies she might need.

When they entered the fourth-grade classroom, Josephine noticed writing on the chalk board. "Doctor Stevens, what is that list for? Are the children in this school all dirty and afraid of getting sick?"

Doctor Stevens smiled and told her to take her pen and notebook and copy the list. They would talk about it when they got home.

The Stevenses were surprised by Josephine's reading. "She reads as well as any adult I know," concluded Doctor Stevens.

Miss Coffee explained when Josephine's mother read aloud every day from the Bible, Josephine sat at her side. Her mother's finger traced underneath the words she was reading. Josephine could read before she went to the one-room schoolhouse in Warren County and read any book she could get her hands on.

Josephine copied the blackboard list and only looked up from her notebook when someone spoke to her. Doctor Stevens stayed with her until noon. He would meet her when school ended for their walk home.

All afternoon, Josephine refused to talk to anyone, to smile or to make eye contact. Part of her plan for reuniting the sisters was to make no new friends in Asheville. Josephine was standing by herself on the playground when Doctor Stevens came to walk her home.

After supper that night, Mrs Stevens took Nora Ann upstairs for her bath and bedtime story. Doctor Stevens and Josephine headed for the library near the front entrance to the house—the first room you saw when you entered. It had one big fancy painting of men on horses, fox hunting with their dogs. Dark mahogany bookshelves lined three sides of the room. One side had medical books, one side was filled with history books; and the third wall had "just great books" according to Doctor Stevens.

An old oak desk, with its own chair and writing tray of pens, pencils and erasers, sat in the middle of the room. "This was my father's desk," Doctor Stevens told Josephine. He was proud to have something of his father's. Josephine told him she understood family treasures. A big brown leather chair occupied a corner with a reading lamp behind it. There were no windows in the room. The light came from the big entrance and the hallway windows by the front door.

Doctor Stevens told Josephine, "My library is your library." He enjoyed her reading and asking him questions. Nora Ann thought the library was too dark and liked spending time in the sunroom with Mrs Stevens. Josephine carried her school notebook and sat at the oak desk after Doctor Stevens had put a pillow on the chair to make her high enough to reach. Doctor Stevens sat in the leather chair and watched as Josephine opened her notebook. He nodded and she read what she had copied from the school black board:

1. I washed my hands before each meal today.

2. I washed not only my face, but my ears and neck, and I cleaned my fingernails today.

3. I kept fingers, pencils, and everything likely to be unclean or injurious out of my mouth and nose today.

4. I brushed my teeth thoroughly after breakfast and after the evening meal today. I took ten or more slow, deep breaths of fresh air today. I was careful to protect others if I spit, coughed, or sneezed.

5. I played outdoors or with open windows more than thirty minutes today.

6. I was in bed ten hours or more last night and kept my windows open.

7. I drank four glasses of water, including a drink before each meal. I drank no tea, coffee, or other injurious drinks.

8. I tried to eat only wholesome food and to eat slowly.

9. I went to toilet at my regular time.

10. I tried hard today to sit up and stand up straight; to keep neat, cheerful, and clean-minded; and to be helpful to others.

11. I took a full bath on each of the days of the week that are checked.

Josephine looked up. Doctor Stevens had settled back into his comfortable chair in the corner. His face was softly lit by the reading lamp. He looked like a doctor and a father who was comfortable at his clinic and his home. Josephine felt tears in her eyes and didn't look up when she finished reading.

Doctor Stevens cleared his throat. "Josephine, those same words are written on every school blackboard in all the schools in this country—rather, in all the schools where the principal cares about the health of his students."

"Are they written on the blackboards at the Appalachian Jackson Orphanage?"

"Absolutely! No one cares more about his students than Doctor Wesler. Why do you think all the doctors and principals in every state want these rules in front of students?"

Josephine thought of Doctor Stevens bringing the clean bedding and taking Mother's body away so quickly. She thought of how it was impossible for her family to do most of the eleven rules. They only had "sponge baths", an outhouse, and if they kept their windows open, they would all freeze in the winter. They did get a lot of fresh air walking to school and helping on the farm. She couldn't remember which classmates washed their pencils and hands in their one-room mountain schoolhouse. She didn't think she ever washed her pencils, but she never put her pencil in her nose or mouth. Her one-room school only had one small blackboard. It could never compare with the resources of the Claxton School. Even though the eleven rules were never on her small blackboard, Josephine knew her teacher cared.

"Do the rules have anything to do with tuberculosis?" she asked.

"You are an excellent student, Josephine. The rules were created so we can prevent the spread of this disease. We want all children and their families to learn the rules. We hope it will keep them well."

Doctor Stevens paused and watched Josephine's face. She looked at him, took a pen from the writing tray on the desk, and began to draw on his list of rules, as Doctor Stevens continued. "If they do get sick, we hope these rules will make them better. Many people with tuberculosis come to Asheville for our fresh mountain air and to benefit from our medical research. Sadly, the only people who can afford our sanitaria and boarding houses have lots of money. We have learned that everyone needs all the fresh air, food, clean habits, and rest they can get, to recover."

Josephine looked up. "It is a wonder that Betty, Pamela, Nora Ann, and I are still alive." Then her anger rose, "Why do you have to be rich to get well? Why don't doctors come and see everyone? Betty had a place for a doctor to stay if they would come and visit Mother. No one ever came."

Doctor Stevens shook his head, "I wish I had answers for your questions, Josephine. It is not fair that your mother did not have a doctor visit her earlier. At our clinic, we are working on finding a cure. Every day in Asheville, we will both be studying—you at Claxton School and I at the Clinic."

Josephine looked at her notebook sitting on the old oak desk. She continued to draw pictures of people with dirty faces looking out of dirty windows. Doctor Stevens watched her in silence. The only sound in the house was Mrs Stevens' voice as she read to Nora Ann.

Josephine's heart ached. It was hard to be mean when the Stevenses were so kind. They would be wonderful parents. Why didn't they want all four sisters? Then Iron Pants emerged, and Josephine nodded as she drew and thought: "I will not be studying at Claxton School, Doctor Stevens. From now on I will only draw sad pictures in my school notebook. I will never copy anything off the blackboard. I will just silently look out the window. When anyone speaks to me, I will look startled, sigh, and say that I was just thinking about my older sisters. Could they repeat what they had just said? I must be with my sisters." Iron Pants had taken over and her words pounded in Josephine's head.

Doctor Stevens straightened up in his chair, "A penny for your thoughts, Josephine." Josephine knew she could not share her thoughts.

She was saved by Mrs Stevens who appeared in the library doorway. "Josephine, it's time for your bath. We can read any book you like before bed. Nora Ann is already in dreamland." Josephine looked at Doctor Stevens sitting in his comfortable chair. His face was troubled, and he had a faraway look in his brown eyes.

She smiled, "I think I will be doing Rule 11, *Full bath on the day of the week that is marked in my calendar.* I also have rules about being a good sister. I will write my sisters every single day. Good night, Doctor Stevens." Doctor and Mrs Stevens looked at each other. Josephine knew that Doctor Stevens was worried. Mrs Stevens had told him about her story with the Little Rabbits and Sister Rich Fox.

On the second day of school, Josephine only drew sad faces in her notebook. Over time, she perfected her dreamy look and did no schoolwork. Josephine knew with time her plan would work.

The months passed quickly, and no one fought with Josephine at Claxton—everyone ignored her. She had no friends. Despite herself Josephine learned a lot. Miss Bean read interesting books to the class, worked out math and science problems on the board, and had everyone but Josephine read the answers to the homework questions.

The eleven rules greeted Josephine every morning and reminded her of what tuberculosis had taken from the four Duke sisters. This memory gave her renewed strength to carry out her plans. It took iron to be mean. She hoped one day she could tell the Stevenses how much she loved and admired them. For now, she would rely on crying, sad pictures and silence.

Asheville North Carolina
Spring 1919

It had been six months since Josephine and Nora Ann had seen Betty and Pamela. The older sisters wrote letters about their lives in the Appalachian Jackson Orphanage. Josephine's letters talked about how she missed her sisters and her bad dreams. Nora Ann drew pictures for each letter sent to Betty and Pamela—pictures of Lazy and Daisy the cats and of all the food on her plate. Nora Ann was "growing like a weed" as their father would have said. A box of letters was no substitute for being with your sisters, Josephine reminded herself.

This morning, Josephine took a new letter from under her pillow. She smiled. The letter was from Miss Bean and addressed to Doctor and Mrs Matthew Stevens. It was not sealed. Josephine had promised Miss Bean she would deliver it. When she was alone waiting for Doctor Stevens to walk her home, she had opened the letter. The letter began:

Josephine is a very bright young girl. We are following your advice, but she seems unhappier each day. Can we schedule another conference?

Josephine held the letter and began to wail. Today would begin with crying, tales of her bad dreams and end with the presentation of the letter.

The Stevenses entered the girls' bedroom as Josephine cried and whispered, "More bad dreams..." While Mrs Stevens patted the crying Nora Ann on the back, Josephine blew her nose and gave the letter to Doctor Stevens. He sat in the rocking chair and read it. Josephine told Mrs Stevens about her bad dream—one where the lace curtains turned into evil fairies that were going to steal her sisters.

Doctor Stevens rocked in his chair as he read. When he finished the letter, he cleared his throat. "Josephine, I have some good news for you. Reverend Miller and Miss Coffee are coming for a visit tomorrow. They will be bringing more news from Betty and Pamela, and some pictures of the new pool at Appalachian."

Josephine watched Mrs Stevens and Nora Ann. They were happy together. She wished she could love Mrs Stevens like a mother, but she had a mother—Patti Duke. Maybe she should just join her sisters and be happy in the orphanage. Never! She could never leave Nora Ann. Josephine's job was to reunite the four sisters. Mrs Stevens looked at Doctor Stevens and turned to Josephine. "Josephine, I will take Nora Ann down to the kitchen. Please get dressed and join us. We are having your favorite pancakes and syrup."

"Thank you, Mrs Stevens. I won't be long. I will make sure to pack a clean hanky for school." Josephine smiled as Doctor Stevens put the letter in his bathrobe pocket and stood up from the rocking chair. He patted Josephine's shoulder as he left with the door still ajar. At the mention of pancakes, Nora Ann had bounded down the stairs ahead of them, turning toward the dining room.

Josephine heard whispering, crept closer to the door and listened. "What do you think David and Mary will be able to do that we can't?" asked Mrs Stevens. "I could not love these girls more if they were my own flesh and blood."

"I know, Sarah. But this constant crying in the morning and Josephine's dreamy behavior in school worries everyone. She spends her days looking out of the window—as if her family would come walking down the streets of Asheville to take her back home. I know she is grieving, but I think maybe the church is right about keeping families together. Let's just have fun today. We will see what happens tomorrow when Reverend Miller and Mary Coffee arrive."

After hearing Doctor Stevens say, "the Church is right about keeping families together," Josephine started getting ready for what she hoped would be her last day of school. She decided to wear the navy-blue dress with the dropped waist and white collar—the first dress Mrs Stevens had given her. She brushed her hair with her mother's old hairbrush and straightened her shoulders. Her mother's brush took the knots out of her hair and out of her thinking.

When Josephine went downstairs, Nora Ann was laughing at Mr Stevens who was playing peekaboo with her, using the morning newspaper. Mrs Stevens had just finished flipping pancakes and was buttering them before she put them on the plates.

The melting butter and maple syrup was so homey. Josephine nodded at Mrs Stevens, took out her hankie, and wiped her right eye. She ate her pancakes, and tried not to look at Doctor Stevens as he played with the paper, and at the laughing Nora Ann.

After breakfast, Josephine kissed Nora Ann goodbye, and left with Doctor Stevens for school. Doctor Stevens had continued to walk Josephine to Claxton School every day. "It's right on my way to the Clinic. Remember we are both learning in Asheville." Doctor Stevens waited until Josephine reached the other children on the playground. She stood apart from the children and watched as he walked down the road toward his clinic.

When the children entered the classroom, Miss Bean complimented Josephine on her nice dress. She had been wearing her old dresses to make sure everyone knew that she didn't really belong in Asheville. Josephine smiled and asked, "May I take my turn at erasing the blackboard and cleaning the chalk erasers this recess?" Miss Bean told Josephine the job was hers, if she promised not to get her new dress soiled.

Josephine looked out the window all morning. Miss Bean did not call on her. Miss Bean dismissed the class for morning recess, leaving Josephine sitting at her desk.

When the classroom was empty, Josephine erased all the blackboards except the one that listed *My Cleanliness Rules*. She was glad that Miss Bean had shortened the longer list she had copied down when she first visited the classroom. After she finished cleaning the erasers, she almost lost her nerve. Then, Iron Pants helped her take the chalk, disguise her handwriting with a messy print style, and write:

My Cleanliness Rules

1. *Wash my hands often*
2. *Brush my teeth*
3. *Comb my hair*
4. *Take my bath often*
5. *Clean my fingernails*
6. *Keep my clothes clean*
7. *Wash my hair weekly*

My Filthiness Rules

1. *Wash my hands weekly*
2. *Have rotten egg breath*
3. *Love your tangles*
4. *Don't take a bath*

5. Pick your nose
6. Never change cloths
7. Greasy hair shine

She drew a picture of a dirty girl with flies circling around her. The girl sat in a mud puddle with a dirty thumb in her mouth. She put down the chalk and erasers and ran out to recess.

When Josephine returned to the classroom with the other students, she went to her desk. As soon as she turned her head, her eyes met Miss Bean who was looking straight at her. The blackboards had been erased clean. It was hard for Josephine to read the look on Miss Bean's face. She nodded at Josephine, and then smiled. Josephine wondered if Miss Bean understood what she had been doing. Did Miss Bean have sisters that she missed? Was she a poor person, living with rich people? She would never know, because if all went as planned this would be her last day in school. Miss Bean had tried, but Claxton School was not the place for Josephine.

When Mrs Stevens and Nora Ann came to get her after school, Josephine rushed out to meet them. She hugged Mrs Stevens and told her she was starved. "Can we go to the drugstore and get a special cookie?"

Nora Ann smiled, pulled Mrs Stevens' hand and said, "Oatmeal raisin, please!" Mrs Stevens and the girls had a great time at the drugstore. Everyone ordered oatmeal raisin cookies. Mrs Stevens was very quiet as they walked home.

Doctor Stevens would not be home for dinner because he had a meeting at his clinic. Mrs Stevens prepared a simple meal of leftover chicken and some nice potatoes and carrots. She mashed the potatoes and carrots together—the way Josephine told her their mother had made them. They had a warm bath with hair washes. Mrs Stevens read a Bible story about Queen Esther and sang a song about how Jesus loved the little children. Then she kissed them and tucked them in together in their single canopy bed. She led them in the Lord's Prayer, and ended with her nightly blessing, "Dear Lord, love and protect our beloved girls."

Josephine wondered if Mrs Stevens ever thought what she would do with the pretty little bedroom if her "beloved girls" left to join their sisters. Did she know that sometimes prayers are not answered the way we want? Josephine was Iron Pants because her prayers were not answered. Even Reverend Miller admitted that while our faith assures us that God will provide, the trouble is God decides what he will provide. Josephine knew she and Nora Ann were supposed to be the answer to the Stevenses' prayers. Her prayer was to reunite with her sisters. God gave her iron to be strong. God would give Mrs Stevens iron when she needed it.

When the sun came through the lace curtains, Josephine was dreaming that Mother was brushing her hair, while Betty and Pamela were reading under a nearby tree. Nora Ann was sleeping on a blanket. It was hard to leave the dream, and the sun's warmth. Then she remembered that this was the day for Reverend Miller and Miss Coffee to arrive. She wiggled and Nora Ann snuggled closer.

"Come on sleepy head, it's time to get up. We have company today. We want to help Mrs Stevens get ready for them." Nora Ann kept her eyes closed and snuggled closer. Josephine heard footsteps on the stairs. The door opened slowly as Mrs Stevens peeked in.

"Good morning, Mrs Stevens," she said, "I was trying to wake up this little snuggle bug. I can't wait for Reverend Miller's and Miss Coffee's visit. I want to see their pictures of Appalachian and get more news of Betty and Pamela."

Mrs Stevens got a faraway look in her eyes as she turned quickly toward the wardrobe. "It would be a good day to wear one of your new dresses." She opened the door. A rainbow of dresses appeared.

"They are lovely, Mrs Stevens, but I still prefer wearing my comfortable dresses—the ones that my mother mended before she got so sick. I think I better wear them before I outgrow them. Your meals are so good. We are getting bigger every day."

"Of course, Josephine, they are all washed and ready. You are old enough to choose your own dress for the day. I will let Nora Ann wear one of the new dresses. Now let's see if we can wake up that little sleepy girl."

After breakfast, Josephine went out on the sunporch to wait for Reverend Miller and Miss Coffee. Doctor Stevens had left to pick them up in his fancy new motor car—a four passenger Sport Touring Roamer that came all the way from Kalamazoo, Michigan. Josephine loved the car's name. She told Doctor Stevens that she admired a car named Roamer from the hometown of Kalamazoo. Doctor Stevens laughed and said he agreed.

Mrs Stevens and Nora Ann found Josephine daydreaming, while she swayed on the wooden glider with the new plaid cushions. "We have about an hour before Reverend Miller arrives," she told Josephine. "Would you like to read a book or tell a story?"

"Oh, Mrs Stevens can we do our tell-and-make-a-play story?"

Even though Mrs Stevens nodded her head and smiled, Josephine saw that her eyes were sad. "What a good idea, Josephine. I bet you even have a new story for us to act out. Nora Ann, how does this sound to you?"

Nora Ann tilted her head and looked from Josephine to Mrs Stevens. "Can I be a robin in your story? I want a nest!"

They went inside to the cozy sitting room with its two clerestory windows, fireplace and small flowered upholstered sofa with a matching love seat. The sitting room and library were Josephine's favorite rooms. She would miss them.

The sitting room adjoined the formal parlor. Josephine never went into the parlor because it felt too imposing. It had large picture windows framed in dark blue velvet drapes. Two sofas and end chairs, covered in gold brocade with gold braid trim, made a box in the middle of the room. Family portraits hung on the walls. A sideboard filled with fancy silver serving dishes faced the end chairs. This room was only used on special occasions.

Josephine remembered Doctor Stevens asking why anyone needed a formal parlor. Mrs Stevens said you could use it when your daughters got engaged or when you entertained their fiancé's family. Doctor Stevens looked puzzled at his wife's response. "Let's not rush through the years, Sarah. We must live each day and see what our little girls teach us. Let's not make any plans beyond a good year at school."

When they were settled in the sitting room, Mrs Stevens took a big square cushion off the flowered loveseat. "Here is a nest for my little robin. Josephine the stage is yours." Mrs Stevens sat on the side of the loveseat that still had a cushion. She reached down and tickled Nora Ann, who did a combination giggle and tweet.

Josephine closed her eyes. This story was one she had been working on for a month. Miss Bean had asked the class to create their own folk tale. Josephine never turned in her story, but she had finally finished it and thought it was as good as any story anyone had read in class. She was sorry that Miss Bean never got a chance to read it.

Josephine stood up, stretched out her arms and began.

Straw Man Learns to See
With Dramatic Embellishments by Mrs Stevens
and Nora Ann

Four robins lived in a nest in a dogwood tree. They had a lovely view of the mountains and were well hidden by the tree's leaves and flowers. Mother Robin kept them warm, and Daddy Robin kept them fed.

One day Mother Robin called Daddy Robin and told him she saw something in the corn field. She didn't know what it was, but she didn't want to fly there until she knew it was safe.

Daddy Robin flew down to the corn field and couldn't believe his eyes. There in the middle of the field was a man made of straw. He had a big straw hat and lots of straw hair. His face was smiling, but nothing on his face moved. "What manner of foolishness is this? I will fly closer and see if I can make this Straw Man blink."

Mrs Stevens began to smile. "Wait a minute, Josephine. I can help with the story. While Nora Ann listens in her nest, I will be the Straw Man. We want to make your story a play!" Mrs Stevens left the room and returned with a broom, big straw hat and a pair of overalls. She pulled lots of her blonde curls down by her face and put on the hat. She stepped into the overalls as she tucked her dress inside. Her pretty pink leather slippers were kicked off and landed against a sofa. After placing the broom on the back of her neck, she put her arms over the broomstick. Mrs Stevens became the Straw Man. Josephine laughed and told the story as Mrs Stevens stood in the middle of the room waving in an imaginary breeze.

Father Robin flew all around the Straw Man. He finally landed on the outstretched arm, hopped closer to the Straw Man's face, and began to nibble his hair. Well, that old Straw Man, doesn't move, and doesn't blink. Father Robin flies straight at Straw Man. Straw Man tosses about in the wind but doesn't blink.

Mrs Stevens moved her arms ever so slightly at the imaginary weight of Father Robin. She kept her eyes frozen wide.

Nora Ann tweeted and giggled in her cushion nest.

Father Robin is getting mad. "Don't just sit there nodding your head. Show me somebody is inside there. Just blink!" Straw Man doesn't move an eye. "You are getting me all in a tizzy, Mr Straw Man. Do you want me to take that funny little eye right out of your head?" Old Straw Man doesn't blink. "Okay, here I come for your shiny eye!"

Father Robin pulls at one eye, but it doesn't come out. He pulls at another eye, and nothing happens. "There is something very funny about your eyes, Mr Straw Man. They remind me of something I use to fasten my shirt. Wait a minute! Who took your eyes, and gave you buttons?"

Straw Man doesn't' blink. He just blows in the wind.

Father Robin begins to think about someone stealing his eyes and giving him buttons. He couldn't see for sure with buttons for eyes. He wouldn't know where to fly, or see his little girlie robins grow up and leave the nest. He is feeling so sad and low. He decides the only place for him is in his nest, with Mother Robin

and the four little girlie robins. He flies straight to his
little nest.

That night, Father Robin tells Mother Robin and
his girlie robins about poor Mr Straw Man and his
button eyes. "I tell you that poor Straw Man can't see
what is right before his eyes. I am feeling so sorry for
him." The End.

"Now, let's really play it," squealed Nora Ann.
"Josephine is Father Robin. But I need three more sister
robins. Where are my sister robins? I have Josephine,
but I want Pamela and Betty! I want four sister robins in
one nest—just like the story and just like at home. Four
girlie robins!"

Mrs Stevens looked at Josephine, tears in her eyes,
but she was still smiling. With a toss of her Straw Man
head, she said, "You are right, Father Robin. I cannot
see what is right before my eyes. The four girlies need
to be in the same nest."

Suddenly the front door opened. Doctor Stevens,
Reverend Miller and Miss Coffee walked into the room.
They looked at Nora Ann in her nest, and Straw Man
Mrs Stevens. Doctor Stevens looked at his wife, "Well,
now. What have we missed?"

Josephine was speechless, but the Straw Man found
her voice, "Well, my dear ones, you missed a wonderful
story. We are just about to act it out. But before we

begin, I need the three of you to sit with Nora Ann on her cushion and pretend to be little girl robins."

Josephine and Mrs Stevens managed to act out the story without tears at the end. The four robins tweeted their hearts out, and even sang a song created by Miss Coffee on the spot.

My little eyes they shine, but they can't help me see.
I only have buttons, don't know what's in front of
me.

When the play was over, Mrs Stevens and Josephine held hands and took a bow. "I love you, Mrs Stevens," Josephine whispered. "I just need to be with my sisters."

"I love you, too, Josephine. I am sorry it took me so long to see. You are the loveliest girls, and I will miss you so."

After their bowing and whispering ended, Mrs Stevens wiped her eyes. She turned to Nora Ann, the men and Miss Coffee—still sitting on the pillow nest. "Well, it is time we got these little girls packed up. It looks like they are traveling with you to Appalachian, Reverend Miller and Miss Coffee. We have learned so much from the wonderful Duke Sisters. I know they will both learn and teach when they join Betty and Pamela at Appalachian."

Doctor Stevens stood up and hugged his wife. Then he looked at Josephine and smiled. He put his arm around Mrs Stevens, "Before we pack, I think we have some eating to do. We don't want to send these robins to bed hungry."

***

Josephine and Nora Ann's last week in Asheville began with packing all their "earthly possessions." Mrs Stevens tried to be brave, and Mr Stevens kept everything as cheerful as he could. They all remembered the best parts of their time together.

Mrs Stevens spoke to the principal at Claxton School, and told him Josephine would be moving to Appalachian, and withdrawing immediately from school. Mrs Stevens told Josephine about her meeting. She recounted all the good things, the principal said about the education at the Appalachian Jackson Orphanage. Josephine realized that it would always be the "orphanage," and not the "school."

The steamer trunks, that had been so empty when the girls arrived in Asheville, were full to bursting with all the clothes, shoes and toys that the Stevenses had bought. Josephine was afraid that the new clothes would set them apart at the orphanage, but she would not do anything to make Mrs Stevens, or herself, sadder.

Josephine looked at the trunks and hugged Mrs Stevens. "I will be so proud to wear these dresses, and then share with the other girls at Appalachian."

When Josephine thought they would all be crushed with sadness, Nora Ann saved them. "Tell me a story. I want it about rabbits. Really funny rabbits!" she demanded. They had been packing books for most of the morning. "Tell it, Josephine. Mrs Stevens and I will watch from my nest."

Mrs Stevens sat on the chair in the girls' room and Nora Ann climbed on her lap. Josephine began to tell a story she had read and rewritten while she was in school. She used her father's humor when she adapted the story and could almost hear his voice when Daddy Rabbit spoke.

Little Rabbit and the Laughing Place

Little Rabbit came to Daddy Rabbit and said, "I want to go where I can learn to laugh. I never laugh. All my brothers and sisters talk about your Laughing Place, and how they all laugh and laugh. They have contests on who can laugh the loudest. I want to go."

Daddy Rabbit looked at his littlest rabbit and thought how serious he was. He and Mrs Rabbit had often talked about how this little rabbit just sat silently and listened, when all the other rabbits were being silly and playing. He hardly ever smiled and never laughed. *"Well, well, Little Rabbit I can take you to the Laughing Place. Do you want to go with all your brothers and sisters, or just with me?"*

This question surprised Little Rabbit. He looked even more serious. "I love going with my brothers and sisters, but I wonder if they would laugh at me if I couldn't laugh loud." Little Rabbit took his hind leg and scratched his long soft ears.

Mrs Rabbit came into the room where Daddy Rabbit and Little Rabbit were looking all serious. "What are you two up to?" They explained about the Laughing Place and the question of who Little Rabbit should take.

Daddy Rabbit smiled and nodded at his wife. "Well, I know one thing. If you take just your sister rabbits, all you need to do is to get one of them laughing, and they will all start. Laughing spreads among girlie rabbits like whooping cough. If one starts laughing, they will all be giggling on the floor in two minutes. Let me show you."

Mrs Rabbit got a funny look on her face, and then began to laugh. Her laughter brought all the girlie rabbits into the room. They stared at her and started to laugh. Mrs Rabbit laughed at the little girl rabbits who laughed at her. They laughed harder and louder. Each giggle caused another one.

Daddy Rabbit looked at his women folk, and slowly moved Little Rabbit to a corner of the room. "Wow! Women folk—laughin' begets laughin'. Glad us men folk aren't like that. When we want to laugh, we just get to burpin' and tootin'. Go get your brother."

Little Rabbit went to the door, and two of his brother rabbits hopped in. They looked at Daddy Rabbit who just spread his legs and let go with one big nasty gas toot! It sounded like a horse fart and who would think a rabbit could make a sound like that? Those two little boy rabbits fell on the floor screaming with laughter. When they caught their breath, they each tooted and began laughing again. They danced and tooted and burped and laughed louder and louder.

What a scene it was in the cabin. Little Rabbit looked to the women who were rolling on the floor laughin' at nothing but laughin'. Then he looked at the men folk dancin' and tootin' and burpin' and laughin' louder and louder.

What happened next? Little Rabbit went from serious, to smiling, and then he began to laugh. The more he looked around the room, the more he laughed. He fell on the floor and laughed until his sides hurt, but he could not stop.

And that's the story of how Little Rabbit found the Laughing Place. The End!

The door opened and Doctor Stevens entered a room full of laughter. Nora Ann said, "Tell me the funny story again!"

"Not until after lunch," said Mrs Stevens. "Let's go wash up and we can have a story for dessert!"

***

For the rest of the week, Nora Ann would stop in the middle of what they were doing and yell, "Laughing Place." Whoever was near her, had to make her laugh. Doctor Stevens did this by making the goofiest faces Josephine had ever seen. He crossed his eyes, used his fingers to stretch his face long and twisted, and messed up his hair. Josephine never knew you could twist your face into so many expressions.

Mrs Stevens and Josephine invented "remember when" stories. "Remember when I was in Doctor Stevens' library and got the book about Grandfather's Tales of North Carolina History? There was a story about the Legend of the White Doe. I got mad that it was about a deer and not about making bread?"

"Yes, but remember how you changed your mind when we discovered that the White Doe was really Virginia Dare?"

Josephine nodded. "Yes, Doctor Stevens and I tried to find out everything about Virginia Dare. We even went to the big library."

"I remember when we used to just grab a book off the shelf and look for the funniest word we could find," said Doctor Stevens.

"Words that just sound funny—Creecy, snuffers, Perquimans, and doggerel buffoonery," Josephine giggled.

Doctor Stevens found his funny words in his medical books. In a book just about ears, noses and throats, he and Josephine found "Pachydermia Larynges", "vaporizing apparatus", and "phlegmonous tonsillitis". When they needed to laugh harder, they made rhymes with the words leachy Creecy, huffer snuffers, or Parchydermia Squirmia Wormia Infirmia.

They went for cookies at the drug store and said goodbye to the nice lady. They drove by the school in the new Touring Roamer automobile and Josephine waved to an empty playground.

Nora Ann asked if Doctor and Mrs Stevens would drive them in the big car to see their sisters. Mrs Stevens took Doctor Stevens' hand and rubbed her eyes as she looked out the window.

"Nora Ann, Miss Coffee and Reverend Miller will be here tomorrow. We will take the four of you to the train station, and they will take you to Appalachian," answered Doctor Stevens.

"To see Betty and Pamela!" sang Nora Ann. "Lazy and Daisy will stay with you, and we will send you pictures."

Josephine thought about what the house would be like for the Stevenses when they were all alone. The storyteller within her began. "Once there was a good man and his loving wife. To the world it looked like they had everything, but they had no children. All they wanted was children."

PART 2

Chapter 8: Trains

King Ferry New York
June 2019

I had just returned from a visit to my natal city, Washington DC. Before me were photos of the house on C Street NE that I lived in for the first two years of my life. I knew my parents would have been proud of how the house had been refurbished from apartments to a single-family dwelling. Trees grew in the yard and the flowers added color from every window box and porch flowerpot.

Much had changed since my parents brought their firstborn daughter home to their C Street apartment in June of 1946. But much had not changed. You could still walk to Union Station and the Mt. Vernon Library from the location. Other ironies were that you could also walk to the Zion Methodist Church and one of the first streets you crossed was North Carolina Avenue. As I walked, every turn led me closer to my mother's past.

Washington DC

June 1941

As the train pulled into Union Station, Josephine searched for her sister. She gathered her new hand-knit green sweater and brown leather handbag off the seat. From the window, a sea of military uniforms greeted her. Josephine smiled as she remembered her sister Nora Ann's letter:

Washington is the place to meet men. There are three guys for every girl in this town. We can't be old maids forever. I can't wait to meet you at the station.

Josephine didn't feel like an old maid. She felt like an accomplished teacher on summer vacation. She loved the struggling school in Cherokee County, North Carolina, where she taught fifth grade. Her salary allowed her to pay down her college loans and still have train fare for a visit to her youngest sister. She wanted to see her sister, and to be close to her hero, First Lady Eleanor Roosevelt. Finding a man was not as exciting as being near the Roosevelts. The New Deal had literally turned on the lights in her school and brought jobs to thousands of poor families who thought they had been forgotten.

An image of a handsome and fatigued President Franklin Roosevelt was on the front page of a newspaper left in the seat next to Josephine. The headline referred to Hitler's gains in Europe. Josephine wondered how long it would be before Nora Ann would be taking care of wounded American soldiers. Even in rural North Carolina, the thought that the United States could not escape the conflict in Europe was discussed and seen as inevitable. Her youngest stepbrother, Robert Edward Duke, was stationed at Pearl Harbor on the USS Arizona. Like Nora Ann, her older sister Betty was an Army nurse. Nora Ann and Betty had been writing weekly about the possible need for nurses able to deploy where they were needed.

As she exited the train, she looked through the crowd for Nora Ann. "Josephine, I'm over here. Come on down. Wake up from your daydreaming. I have someone I want you to meet." Josephine ran toward her sister, and they hugged.

The man at Nora Ann's side stood back. He was of average height and looked fit in his army dress uniform. He had lively brown eyes and a smile that would make any woman turn his way. He smiled as he watched the reunited sisters. They stood about five feet two with brown hair curled and waved in the style of the time. Their blue eyes closed as they embraced.

His handsome face and smile stopped more than a few nurses in the crowd. They moved on when they saw that he was clearly with the two women with the lilting

Southern voices and hugging ways. He was startled by Nora Ann's voice. "Cleo, stop your daydreaming. I want you to meet my sister Josephine. She came all the way from North Carolina to shake your hand."

Cleo quickly moved closer to the Duke sisters and offered his hand to Josephine. "I am delighted to meet you. I'm sure you came to see your sister, not me. We all love Nora Ann's storytelling."

Josephine relaxed as he spoke. She smiled and took his hand. "I am delighted to meet you. I agree. Nora Ann is a great teller of tales."

Nora Ann nodded her head and faked a frown. "Well, this teller of tales is hungry. Cleo has promised us dinner with four of his finest fellow soldiers. Lead on Sergeant Piatt." Nora Ann placed her arm through Cleo's and urged Josephine to do the same. Josephine smiled up at Cleo as she held his arm. There was something about this man she liked, and his smile made her feel flirtatious.

Asheville Train Station North Carolina
Spring 1919

Josephine finished her big hug with Mrs Stevens and gave Doctor Stevens a version of one of his goofiest faces. He appreciated her effort and returned with a very goofy face of his own.

Reverend Miller shook his head and smiled. Miss Coffee continued to hug Mrs Stevens. It was a hug that comforted and helped her stand up at the same time. Josephine knew that the only way to make the day work was to look forward, not backward. Nora Ann was mesmerized by the train and had no trouble looking forward.

Josephine watched the train approach and then walked back to Mrs Stevens. She thought she had finally found the words for their goodbye.

She put out her arms for another hug and said softly, "Not goodbye, we love you and…" Josephine had words and then lost them. She was going to say that she knew Mrs Stevens would one day be a mother, but she could not say them. It was like saying that their mother loved them too much to die. There are some promises you can't make, even to people you love.

Lost in thought with her sentence unfinished, Josephine heard Reverend Miller. "The race does not always go to the swift, but the train will definitely leave the slow at the station. Come on girls. I promised your sisters we would get you to Appalachian Jackson Orphanage before the snow falls."

Mrs Stevens gave Josephine another big hug and said, "Not goodbye and know we love you." Miss Coffee took her hand. With one last look over her shoulder at Doctor and Mrs Stevens, Josephine headed to the train platform. She walked up the stairs onto the nearest train car. Miss Coffee lifted Nora Ann up to her. Reverend Miller joined them and held Miss Coffee's hand as she entered the car. The train whistle blew. They were leaving Asheville and the Stevenses. The four sisters would soon be together—four girlie robins in the same nest.

***

Reverend Miller held their train tickets in his hand, as they walked through crowded train cars. Within seconds, a conductor took the tickets and led them to the fanciest passenger car—the one next to the dining car. Josephine remembered that the Stevenses had bought the tickets and guessed that this would be the last time any of them were seated in the most expensive and elegant train car. Reverend Miller thanked the conductor as they settled into the soft leather seats. Nora quickly fell asleep with her head on Miss Coffee's lap.

Josephine looked out of the train window as they headed east to Appalachian. As they moved from city to country and the mountain shadows lengthened, her mind wandered to Daniel Boone. Miss Bean had read a book about Daniel Boone when Josephine first came to the Claxton School. Even though she had out her hankie and her head on the book, Josephine was hooked on every word of the story. She remembered Boone talking about how he would watch the sun go down over the mountains and felt that freedom lay to the west—toward the sunset. Daniel Boone said that when he looked west, he heard a horn of freedom blowing.

Miss Coffee was reading a book about how the railroad was made so people could travel west. Josephine didn't have a book to read so she just looked out the window. As the train rattled forward and the train car moved rhythmically side to side, her eyes got heavy. She snuggled close to Miss Coffee and was almost asleep when Reverend Miller whispered to Miss Coffee. Josephine struggled to keep her breathing slow and deep, eyes relaxed and ears on high alert. "Are they both asleep?" whispered Reverend Miller.

Josephine could hear the smile in Miss Coffee's voice, "Like two little angels."

"When should we tell them about our wedding?" asked Reverend Miller.

"Let's tell them when we eat dinner. The dining car is just the perfect place for our announcement," said Miss Coffee.

There was silence and then Miss Coffee whispered, "How are the four boys who lost their parents in the horse carriage accident? Have you found any relatives to care for them? They are all just babies. What will your church be able to provide?" Josephine could imagine her sad eyes and frown from her new tone of voice.

There was a long pause. Reverend Miller replied, "Well, the Reilly's don't have much of a horse, but they have strong hearts. They took in the boys. We are still hoping to find some relatives. You did a wonderful job with your four Duke girls, but you need to get back to school."

Miss Coffee was quiet. Josephine's mind jumped and words screamed in her head, "Ask Doctor and Mrs Stevens if they want four boys! They can love better than anyone."

Miss Coffee seemed to be reading her mind. "Is it too early to talk to Matt and Sarah Stevens about these boys? I am not sure their family would approve of four rollicking boys from Warren County after the two cantankerous Duke girls from the same region. But no one can deny that they have proved themselves the most loving parents."

"Matt Stevens already knows about the boys. I asked for his help when we had to visit the children. I still struggle with how you explain to young children what happened to their parents and why we need to take them from their home. It was a hard trip to the Reilly's farm. I did take your suggestion to have each boy bring something from home that they loved—well it was only the oldest boy who understood. He gathered things for his three brothers."

"Matt has a friend, Daniel Evans, who works in a new clinic in Warren County. Doctor Evans visited the Reilly family and examined the boys. They are healthy, but very confused. Matt knows we need to find a family quickly."

Suddenly the train whistle blared, signaling their arrival at the next station. The whistle woke Nora Ann who bolted upright. Josephine pretended to wake up and wiggled away from Miss Coffee's side. Nora Ann snuggled next to Miss Coffee for a moment then declared that she was starving.

Josephine rubbed her eyes, stretched, and agreed that she could use some food, too. "Let's head to the dining car," said Reverend Miller. "I think we will all be delighted with what we find on the menu."

"What's a menu?" asked Nora Ann.

"What a good question, Nora Ann. A menu is a list of foods that you can choose for your meal. It is often a printed list that is divided into different meals like breakfast, lunch and dinner." Miss Coffee's voice changed from Nice Friend to Teacher with a Lesson.

Nora Ann looked confused. "I can only choose ice cream—strawberry is my favorite. Oh, I can choose cookies, oatmeal raisin, please."

Miss Coffee looked at Reverend Miller, who was trying to lead the way to the dining car, then returned to her lesson on menus. "I don't have my trusty Merriam-Webster dictionary with me. I think the word was French, but like so many of our words began with a Latin root."

"Trees have roots," said Nora Ann.

Reverend Miller took Miss Coffee's hand, "I have an idea, let's keep walking and see what a menu looks like. Then we can talk about the history of the word, and the meaning of roots. We can learn better on a full stomach."

When they entered the dining car, Nora Ann shrieked, "Look at all the hats. We all have hats!" The elegant tables and window booths were set with white linen tablecloths, silverware and napkins folded into triangles sitting on small plates. Then Nora Ann whispered, "Why are the glasses upside down?"

"The glasses are upside down to prevent dust from getting inside. They stay clean until they pour us water before our meal," explained Miss Coffee. "Let's select a place and watch our nice waiter turn over the glasses and bring us our menus," she said.

Reverend Miller chose a booth by the window. He motioned Nora Ann and Josephine to sit together with Nora Ann nearest the window. Miss Coffee slid in opposite Nora Ann. With a seamless motion Reverend Miller sat beside her and took her hand.

Before Reverend Miller could speak, Nora Ann took a folded napkin and put it on her head. A handsome waiter in a white coat and black bowtie walked to the table. When he saw Nora Ann, his passive black face cracked into a smile. Then in an instant, the smile disappeared—his face again unreadable. He handed everyone a menu—giving Nora Ann her menu last. She was sitting ramrod straight so her "hat" would not fall off. Again, Josephine saw a flicker of a smile in his eyes as he looked at Nora Ann.

"Thank you so much," said Reverend Miller to the waiter. "It might take us a while to decide on our dinner order. The girls have never eaten in a dining car before or had a menu."

"I understand, sir. I will give you all the time you need."

Nora Ann struggled to sit still and keep her hat balanced. When she saw Miss Coffee take her napkin "hat", unfold it and place it in her lap, she exclaimed, "It's a napkin for your lap? I can do that." In a flash the hat was off her head and a napkin in her lap. Nora Ann looked around the dining car.

Two very stylish women with cloche hats and fur neckpieces sat in the booth facing Nora Ann. One hat was a deep rose—Nora Ann's favorite color. "There's a pink hat…not a napkin for your lap. I love pink hats."

As Nora Ann watched, the woman with the rose-colored cloche opened her purse, retrieved a cigarette, gold lighter and a long ivory and gold holder. She placed the cigarette in the holder, lit it and watched as the smoke curled from the end of the cigarette.

Nora Ann froze for a moment and then began to push against Josephine yelling, "Smoking stick! Fire!"

Reverend Miller and Miss Coffee whipped around toward the women. Instantly Miss Coffee turned back, put her finger to her lips, and whispered, "Hush." Reverend Miller guffawed. When he tried to swallow his laugh, he had a coughing fit. Miss Coffee lifted her glass of water to hand to Reverend Miller at the moment Nora Ann bumped her shoulder. Her water spilled all over Reverend Miller who just coughed and laughed louder.

The waiter was almost at the table but had to turn around to hide another grin. When Josephine put her hand over her mouth to stop laughing, she dropped her menu. The waiter approached her to pick up the fallen menu. He carried new napkins for the spilled water. As he lifted the menu from the carpet, their eyes met and flashed laughter. His face settled into unreadable again, while tears of laughter-streaked Josephine's face and her chest shook with swallowed giggles.

Things calmed down as Miss Coffee read the menu. She explained that cigarettes were just like Daddy's pipes that burned tobacco and made smoke. "Sometimes people put their cigarettes in fancy holders and that makes them look long like a stick. What should we order?"

Nora Ann asked about everything on the menu. Then they settled for familiar favorites—salt pork, mashed potatoes and chocolate cake.

After dinner, Reverend Miller and Miss Coffee told the girls that they would be getting married in June. All four of the Duke girls would be attending—another gift from the Stevens' family. Nora Ann asked questions about weddings, and if they would take a train ride to the wedding.

Miss Coffee patiently answered her while Reverend Miller and Josephine made sure every crumb of chocolate cake was devoured.

As they settled back in their train car, Josephine picked up Miss Coffee's book. "Can I look at your book? I am already missing the Stevenses' library."

Miss Coffee nodded yes. She held Reverend Miller's hand, leaned her head on his shoulder, and closed her eyes. Josephine encouraged Nora Ann to see how many stars she could count from the moving train. She hoped counting stars would be like counting sheep and make Nora Ann drowsy. She wanted to be all alone with the book.

Miss Coffee had marked her page with a Bible verse bookmark. Josephine began reading the history of the North Carolina railroads going west. She looked at the pictures, and then went to the bookmarked page. The chapter described the labor used by Pullman and Company—predominantly black convicts dressed in striped, yellow garb. They slept in cramped prison cars without air or light and worked from sunup to sundown in filthy conditions. Many of them died working on the railroads.

Josephine wanted to get the image of the car packed with men who couldn't move or breathe out of her mind. She thought of the nice waiter and wondered if someone in his family was forced to lay down railroad tracks. She wondered if the waiter was an orphan who questioned why his parents died working for a rich man's railroad. Did he feel sad that his nice job was built on the bones of his ancestors?

Sadly, she knew she could not ask the waiter—they lived in the South. Even the orphanages kept the races separate. Didn't they realize that orphans had a bond that would draw them together?

That night, Nora Ann and Josephine slept in the same bunk. Miss Coffee was in the bunk below them in the sleeper car. Reverend Miller slept in his seat. They traveled all night. The sun rose just as they arrived at the Appalachian station. Josephine and her sisters would be together by nightfall.

Chapter 9: Nicknames

King Ferry New York
June 2019

The good thing about the name Elaine is that it is very difficult to turn into a nickname. My mother never liked nicknames. As a child, I thought that was because all our neighbors called my mother Jo for Josephine. They called my father Cleo. When they were introduced for the first time, everyone thought my father was Joe and my mother was Cleo. I thought this was funny, but my mother disagreed. "I am not as fussy about nicknames as when I was a child. But sometimes folks should know when to call you by your family-given name. I don't mind 'Cleo,' but 'Jo and Josie' have always set me off."

Washington DC
June 1941

Cleophas walked Josephine and Nora Ann home after their dinner. He promised to call before he left for Fort Meade the next day.

Inside the apartment, Josephine asked Nora Ann to tell her more about this attractive young soldier. Nora Ann sat back in her chair. "Did Cleo tell you he was the captain of his high school football team, and had a college scholarship?" Josephine shook her head. "Well, no money at home, meant no college. So off he goes to Washington DC to find a job and then the Army found him."

"The first thing I asked him was, who in the world named him Cleophas? Cleo laughed and told me about his mother Sarah—known to most of her friends as Sally."

Nora Ann jumped out of her chair and in her best Cleo voice continued, "After my mother had her first child, Ellen, she got religion. She decided to name the rest of her children from the Bible—so we had Joseph and Daniel. Sadly, the Easter before I was born, my mother was struck by the gospel of Luke. Luke described the resurrected Jesus meeting two disciples on their way to Emmaus. The disciple, Cleophas, was one of the first, besides the women at the tomb, to recognize Jesus back from the dead. Mother wanted her children holy, and we tried—some of us harder than others." Nora Ann took a little bow. Josephine longed to meet Cleo's mother, and his brothers and sisters.

The apartment was small with one bed that Josephine and Nora Ann shared. As they settled in,

Josephine treasured the closeness of her sister. She tried to calm her mind and sleep—but she kept thinking about the nicknames in Cleophas' family. Cleo, Dan and Joe were nicknames, as was his mother's Sally for Sarah. Josephine was wary of people who gave you nicknames, and she knew why.

Instead of sleeping, she returned to the Appalachian Jackson Orphanage. The battle of nicknames with her cottage mother Miss Faircloth was in full swing. For someone who did not like wars, Josephine could draw a line and choose her battle. It was time to fight once more.

Appalachian Jackson Orphanage
Spring 1919

Josephine and Nora Ann settled into the same cottage with Betty and Pamela at Appalachian Jackson Orphanage when they were reunited after leaving Asheville. There were twelve girls in the cottage. Nora Ann was the youngest and Helen, a senior in high school, the oldest. They lived together in an open room with twelve beds of the same size. Nora Ann had all the room in the world, while Helen's feet hung over the edge of her bed. Miss Faircloth, their cottage mother, had an alcove for privacy, but shared the same cottage.

The first time Nora Ann saw her older sisters, she shouted, "Where is your hair?" Betty picked her up and twirled her around and explained that everyone got a special haircut when they came to Appalachian Jackson Orphanage and that she and Josephine would get one the next day. "I don't want a haircut," whined Nora Ann. Josephine decided she would be a good example to her little sister and not complain about the haircut. She didn't want a fight now that she was finally reunited with her older sisters. She was sure she could soothe Nora Ann the next day.

Miss Faircloth called from her alcove, "Josie, it's time for your new haircut." Josephine rounded the alcove corner, nodded at Miss Faircloth, and put her hands on her hips. "My mother named me Josephine. Josie is not a real name. If I gave myself a name, it would be Iron Pants."

Miss Faircloth motioned Josephine to take a chair and began to cut her hair with kitchen scissors and a bowl. After parting Josephine's hair down the middle, she combed the hair. Using the bowl to guide her, she cut a straight line for the bangs. Next the bowl was used to complete the cut at the neckline. Josephine's hair barely covered her ears. Miss Faircloth sighed. "What do you think of your new haircut, Josie?"

"My name is not Josie. My mother named me Josephine, and she called me Josephine. The reason we are at this orphanage is that our mother is dead, and so is our father. If you insist on calling me Josie—then please call me Josie Iron Pants—this is a name I have given myself."

Miss Faircloth did not respond. She took the towel from around Josephine's neck, dusted off her collar, and began to sweep up the hair.

Josephine hated nicknames. Your name was given to you by the only people who have a right to name you—your mother and father. Miss Faircloth needed to remember her Bible and honor everyone's mother and father.

Miss Faircloth sighed again. "Well, Josie, your hair is nice and neat. You look like all the little girls in our cottage. Go and get your little sister Annie for her haircut."

"Her name is Nora Ann, Miss Faircloth. That is the name our mother and father gave her. Whenever we would walk into town, the folks used to say, 'Here come those pretty little Duke girls.' Our parents were very proud of us."

Suddenly, Miss Faircloth looked like life as a cottage parent might not be her favorite job. In a blink, Josephine recognized sympathy in Miss Faircloth's eyes and wondered if she really liked girls who spoke their mind. Did she hate nicknames, too?

As Josephine stared at the cottage-mother's face, she noticed how young and pretty Miss Faircloth was. Her hair was tied back straight and plain, and she wore a simple sack dress and a worn sweater. Did Miss Faircloth like being a mother hen for the twelve girls in her cottage?

Josephine wanted to make her cottage-mother smile—maybe even laugh. She thought she could ask Miss Faircloth if she had a nickname. She might even suggest her nickname could be "Miss Pretty Dress." This made Josephine grin. No one had a pretty dress at the Orphanage. All the clothes had the color washed out and the wrinkles renewed as they were thrown in a pile for orphan wardrobes.

Josephine brushed the hair off her sack dress while Miss Faircloth took all the hair she had swept outside, "for the birds to build their nests." When she returned, they watched the birds swoop down on the pile of hair, flying away with full beaks. "Miss Faircloth, do you know where the birds are building their nests?"

Miss Faircloth got a very wistful look on her face. "Oh, Josephine, I wish I had time to follow them and find out. When I was little, my first book was *The Birds of North Carolina*. My grandmother and I would spend hours walking and looking at birds, learning their names, and finding their nests. I still know the names of all the birds."

"I would love to learn all the names of the birds. Maybe you could teach me." Josephine and Miss Faircloth looked at each other.

Miss Faircloth pursed her lips. "I think we will be learning the Bible before our birds." Josephine nodded and told Miss Faircloth that she would bring Nora Ann for her haircut. As Josephine walked out the door, she froze in her steps. She heard Miss Faircloth whisper to herself, "Good-bye Josie Iron Pants." And then the cottage mother laughed—really laughed.

When Josephine got to the cottage, Nora Ann was sitting on her bed looking out the window. "Do you like my new haircut?" Nora Ann looked at Josephine's face and put her hand up to feel the bangs.

Suddenly Josephine spied Miss Faircloth standing in the door. She didn't look her way, just pretended she and Nora Ann were alone. "Nora Ann, today we are getting new haircuts and old dresses. This is my haircut done with a bowl over the head and blunt scissors."

Nora Ann continued to run her fingers around the ends of Josephine's bobbed hair. She laughed when Josephine made a funny face like she was tickling her. Aware of her audience in the doorway, Josephine continued, "But luck is with us. Even with new haircuts and old dresses, we get to keep the names that our mother and father gave us. What is my name?"

"Josephine Helen Duke," said Nora Ann.

"What is your name?" asked Josephine.

"Nora Ann Duke," said Nora Ann.

Miss Faircloth cleared her throat. They turned to her in the doorway. Josephine tried to look surprised. "Nora Ann, it is time for your haircut. Josephine, you can come with your little sister if you want. We will finish before lunch, and we can go and meet Pamela and Betty in the lunchroom."

As Nora Ann was getting her bowl haircut, Josephine stood by the window of the cottage. She heard the whistle of a train speeding by on the tracks to the north of the campus. She wondered if they were on the right or the wrong side of the tracks. Southerners cared a lot about what side of the tracks you were from. When Josephine thought of their old farm in the mountains to the north, she was pretty sure folks thought that they were on the wrong side of the tracks—dirt poor farmers. Josephine thought of her mother and father and wondered how you learned to keep sadness at bay. How do people move forward—tracks or no tracks?

Josephine watched Nora Ann's lovely auburn hair piling on the floor. Her thoughts shifted to summer days when their Mother would dry her hair outside in the sunshine. Mother would sit on a fallen log and let the breezes dry her waist length hair. Josephine would sit down and lay her head on Mother's lap. Josephine could

almost feel her Mother stroking her hair while she
sang…

Sometimes I feel like a motherless child,
Sometimes I feel like a motherless child
Sometimes I feel like a motherless child
A long way from my home

Josephine wondered if Mother was a fortune teller. Did
she know all her girls would one day be motherless? It
was such a beautiful song. She would never have a
chance to ask Mother where she learned her songs and
stories. She would never be able to ask her how she felt
when she knew she was dying.

Josephine's daydreaming ended with the crash of
the stool as Nora Ann jumped down after her haircut
yelling, "Let's go eat! I want to see Betty and Pamela.
Do I get a special lunch, Miss Faircloth? I was a good
haircut sitter."

Miss Faircloth offered Nora Ann her hand. "Come
this way and let's find your sisters. We can eat together
before they go to class. Let's not worry about special
food today."

As they walked outside to meet Betty and Pamela,
Josephine hummed *Motherless Child*. To her surprise,
Miss Faircloth started singing:

Sometimes I wish, I could fly, like a bird up in the sky,
Sometimes I wish, I could fly, like a bird up in the sky little closer to home

Miss Faircloth stopped, looked over to the cottage, to the pile of hair where three birds had landed. "Girls, those are robins. I am sure you know that. Last year, two built a nest in the apple tree in back of the library. Did you know that robins always have four eggs in their nest? The mother does not sit on the nest until four eggs are there."

Nora Ann looked up and smiled. "Our Momma didn't stop until she had four eggs—four little girl eggs. Josephine and I know a story about four little girl robins. Josephine is a good storyteller."

Miss Faircloth knelt and gave Nora Ann a big hug. "Yes, Nora Ann, your mother had four nice little girls— Betty, Pamela, Josephine and Nora Ann. I hope Josephine will tell us her story about the robins some evening. We mountain folk are good storytellers."

Josephine had picked the right battle. Honoring your name and understanding the new adults in your life matter. You must also honor those who have iron in their veins. There was iron in Miss Faircloth.

Chapter 10: Libraries and Mr Harris

King Ferry New York
September 2019

My earliest memory of being in a library was at the age of six. I was with my parents and five-year-old brother Carl in the Library of Congress. We were attending a special holiday concert at the invitation of a friend of my parents, Minnie Elmer. Minnie worked at the Library of Congress and had lived next to Mother on C Street during the war. We watched Minnie's string quartet perform in the Library's grand foyer. Minnie was the first librarian I ever met, and I hold all others to her standard.

The first standard is that only knowledge counts—appearances are superfluous. Minnie was tall and thin. If Abraham Lincoln had a twin sister, she would have looked exactly like Minnie—craggy face, dark hair and eyes that gleamed when she talked. Her voice was so low that it rumbled. Minnie knew all about the music she cataloged for the library. She even went to other countries to make sure she was getting all her facts straight.

The second standard is librarians must be good storytellers. As a child when I sat on Minnie's lap to listen to her stories, her thin chest vibrated just like the cello she played. My favorite Minnie story was one that she told me when I was in college. I called it, *Minnie in Italy*. I always hear her low, resonating, musical voice when I think of her words.

The only time I don't want to be in Italy is when I am packing to go there. I have special dresses that roll into little bags. They never wrinkle. But I do hate packing a suitcase. So many things to remember.

I always stay in the same hotel in Sicily. The first time I stayed there I discovered the closet had no hangers for my dresses. I hated to bother the concierge, so I just bought five hangers. When it was time to leave, I left them in the closet for the next guest.

Two years later, I returned to Sicily and this hotel. The clerk greeted me and gave me a room key. I had no more than put my suitcase down when there was a knock on the door. I opened it to see the concierge holding my five hangers wrapped in a ribbon. 'Here you are dear Miss Elmer. We saved these hangers for your return. We have missed you.' I took them with tears in my eyes. The hotel suddenly felt like home.

Washington DC
June 1941

Josephine and Nora Ann made a quick breakfast of oatmeal and toast before Nora Ann left for the Army hospital. Left to her own devices, Josephine decided to walk back to Union Station and buy a newspaper to catch up on Eleanor Roosevelt's *My Day* columns. She first started reading *My Day* in 1935 as a college junior at Appalachian State Teachers College in Boone, North Carolina. She never wanted to miss a day with Eleanor who was now the First Lady of the land. June's *My Day* columns had begun with Eleanor and her friend driving through Washington DC, New York and New England. Josephine wanted to be with her favorite traveler.

Daydreaming as she walked, Josephine saw herself in the car with Eleanor. If they talked too much, they might forget a turn and get lost, but she wouldn't care. The journey would be enough. Josephine imagined the air getting colder as they drove north and wondered who they would meet when they stopped for the night.

The sound of a car horn brought Josephine back to the streets of Washington DC. She stopped and looked up and down. C Street and Union Station had disappeared. The street she walked down was lined with small houses and apartments ending with a large building, hopefully with someone to direct her.

Approaching the structure, she smiled. She would be spending the morning with Eleanor—at the library.

Entering the Carnegie Library, she read a plaque that acknowledged Andrew Carnegie for funding the library. Next to the plaque was a photo of President Theodore Roosevelt at the library dedication in 1903.

Josephine enjoyed telling her students stories of the Roosevelt family. She explained that Teddy Roosevelt was Eleanor Roosevelt's uncle and that the current President Franklin Roosevelt was Eleanor's husband. In her best teacher voice, Josephine described how Eleanor grew up in a family that cared about politics, public service and running for office—ending with the Presidency. Josephine proposed that Eleanor understood how the world could move toward peace and justice and that Eleanor inspired her husband Franklin and the nation. Many of her students looked puzzled, but some nodded in agreement. Some were learning to love Eleanor as much as their pretty young teacher, Miss Duke.

A sign directed Josephine to the newspapers. In minutes, a well-dressed young man handed her a stack of newspapers. "I have gathered all the *My Day* columns you wanted, from June 4 to today."

Josephine looked at his neatly pressed shirt and dark tie. "Thank you so much. Can you show me the way to the reading room?"

Following the young librarian into the reading room, Josephine settled near a window with a view of the Washington Monument. Her comfortable leather chair and side table allowed her to put down her purse and the pile of newspapers. She thanked the young librarian and watched as he returned to his desk in the newspaper section.

Josephine's favorite time in the orphanage had been in the library. Mr Harris, the school librarian, was always nicely dressed, and able to find a book you would love in an instant. Mr Harris was the one who told Josephine that Eleanor Roosevelt was an orphan when she asked if only poor children lost their parents. Mr Harris answered questions honestly and he knew that certain experiences would change you forever.

Appalachian Jackson Orphanage
June 1919

Even though it was summer, Pamela and Betty and other older students went to school as well as work. Pamela and Betty worked in the afternoon and had school in the morning. Josephine and Nora Ann had school in the morning and reading in the afternoon. They joined their sisters for lunch every day.

As Josephine and Nora Ann walked from their morning classes to the dining hall, Josephine appreciated her short haircut and threadbare dress. The day was already hot and humid, and she was starting to sweat. When they entered the dining hall, Nora Ann ran over to the table where Betty and Pamela were sitting. Josephine followed and they all sat down.

Pamela was complaining to Betty, "Why do we get the hot afternoons for work and not the nice cool classroom? It's not fair!" Pamela was very pretty, even when she was complaining.

Betty looked bewildered, "We were always taught not to complain because it was rude, and it didn't work. That said, complaining seems to work very well for you, Pamela." Josephine agreed. Pamela had complained about her clothes, and suddenly she had the prettiest of the silly sack dresses and the nicest of the second-hand straw hats.

While Pamela ranted about how she disliked her work in the laundry, Josephine began to daydream about her sisters. Even though Betty was the oldest, she and Pamela were the same size. Betty could never hope to match Pamela in beauty, but she would always be the kindest one. Betty's eyes were clear and realistic with a slight hint of optimism. Pamela was charming and when she knew what she wanted, her blue eyes were a lethal weapon. Josephine knew that she needed to keep her eyes open to learn from her surroundings. Sometimes she tried to squint and look skeptical. Nora Ann still had little girl eyes—eyes that showed hope and flashed her frequently changing emotions.

Josephine had seen sadness in all their blue eyes. Josephine wondered if Betty's grief could be the hardest because she had known Mother the longest—for fifteen years. Then Josephine remembered Nora Ann's whimpering last night in bed and her asking for Momma. All their blue eyes revealed that they were all longing for their mother.

A ringing bell startled Josephine from her daydream. She was back in the dining room as Miss Faircloth asked them to bow their heads for grace. No grace, no food was the policy. Betty, Pamela, Nora Ann and Josephine all held hands, as the grace was said:

God our Father, Lord and Savior,
Thank you for your love and favor
Bless this food and drink we pray
And all who share with us today. Amen.

When the grace was finished, Josephine whispered just loud enough for Betty, Pamela and Nora Ann to hear, "And God bless our angel mother." Then all four Duke girls said, "Amen."

During lunch, Pamela continued complaining. "It is horrible. We take the clothes and linens down from the lines and fold them for each cottage. You cannot imagine how irritating it is to work with such sad, sad, clothing. They are all faded, shapeless and scream that someone else had worn them before and someone would grow into them and wear them again and again until they become rags. That's kind of a joke because really they are rags now—and I am not talking glad rags."

Pamela hated that Betty put up with the laundry work. She did not seem to mind working with the rags and even hummed as she folded clothes.

Betty listened patiently and looked at the clock on the wall. "Time for work," she chirped. Pamela kept complaining and Betty left for the laundry by herself.

Josephine watched Pamela as Betty left the lunchroom. Josephine's eyes followed Pamela's gaze. Miss Faircloth was waving to a new teacher—a short, bald man with a round tummy. He had round wire glasses and looked like he was more bothered by the heat than anyone on campus. He had a nice white handkerchief that he kept taking from his shirt pocket and wiping his forehead. It made his bald head look even shinier.

Pamela moved over to stand near Miss Faircloth. She arrived just as Miss Faircloth said, "Welcome, Mr Harris. It is surely a warm day." Pamela waved for Josephine and Nora Ann to join her. She grabbed their hands and smiled her sweetest smile. Her sisters smiled and waited for clues.

Mr Harris smiled, wiped his forehead, and then took off his glasses and polished them. "It is a pleasure to be here, regardless of the temperature. I have waited so long for a school to offer me the job of librarian as well as history teacher. Being here is a dream come true," he said with a slight bow. Josephine smiled and thought that wherever Mr Harris grew up, chivalry was not dead.

Mr Harris had a bag that was overflowing with books. One had just fallen out of the bag and Pamela swept down like a falcon to pick it up. "Oh, Mr Harris," she said with a smile that would melt butter, "Let me help you. My sisters and I love books and have been just waiting for our new librarian. We had hoped that we could be chosen to work with you in the new library. There is so much to be done. Have any students been assigned to assist you?" Again, Pamela smiled and tilted her head just a little to the left as her gaze met Mr Harris' eyes.

"Oh, where are my manners?" she cooed. "Let me introduce myself. I am Pamela Duke and I live in Miss Faircloth's cottage with my three sisters. I am pleased to introduce you to my younger sisters, Josephine and Nora Ann." Nora Ann and Josephine politely shook hands with Mr Harris. He seemed very glad to meet the girls. Miss Faircloth stood off slightly to the side. She too was caught up in Pamela's little drama. Both

Josephine and Miss Faircloth suspected that Pamela had a plan.

Mr Harris offered to take the book that Pamela was holding. She flashed her movie star smile, "I wouldn't dream of not helping you with these books. In fact, please give me some more and let Josephine and Nora Ann carry some as well."

Mr Harris gave another slight bow, "I so appreciate some help. Would this be acceptable, Miss Faircloth?"

As Josephine watched Miss Faircloth, she saw a flicker in Miss Faircloth's eyes. Yes, there it was again. She was amused! Just as quickly, her stern cottage-mother face returned, "That would be fine, Mr Harris. The Duke sisters are a formidable team. They will be a great help, I am sure."

Pamela, Josephine and Nora Ann walked to the library with Mr Harris. When they got there, he handed Pamela the key that she immediately placed in the lock and opened the door. She stood back, but Mr Harris bowed again and said, "Ladies first."

The library smelled of new wood and the windows were sparkling clean. The new bookshelves were empty while the tables and floors were covered with boxes of books. Josephine smiled at all the books. Nora Ann was happy to be a big girl helper. Pamela tossed her head and seemed to be breathing in the cool of the library.

Mr Harris looked at the three sisters and at the books. Then he pulled out his handkerchief and to the girls' great surprise dabbed at a tear in his eyes. They stopped smiling and even Pamela looked worried. "Oh, girls, please forgive me," said Mr Harris. "Seeing you standing before me makes me think of my family in Atlanta and especially of my four little sisters. For a moment, I got so homesick. How silly of me to cry," he whispered and put away the handkerchief and smiled at the girls.

"There is no one in North Carolina who understands what it is like to be homesick and miss your family more than the three of us," Josephine assured Mr Harris. "And no one wants more than we do to help you get our new library ready."

"Well, Miss Pamela, Miss Josephine and Missy Nora Ann, you are right. It is time to get to work." And so, the sisters' new lives as official library helpers began. They unboxed books as Mr Harris began to put them in order to place on the library shelves. Pamela could now sing as she worked. She was out of the heat and rags and into the afternoon work that others would envy.

Later that day, Mr Harris officially talked to Doctor Wesler and Miss Faircloth about needing library helpers. Pamela stood up for Betty and was only slightly smug when she told Betty that they were out of the laundry and the sisters would spend their afternoons with Mr Harris in the cool of the library. Betty laughed at the news, "Wow, I would willingly trade the wet wash for some beautiful books. Can you give me some lessons in complaining, Pamela?" All three sisters laughed until they couldn't get their breath and then Josephine snorted. Laughter still begets laughter with the girls.

***

In less than a week, about a quarter of the library books were shelved. Josephine worked shelving and dusting, while Nora Ann "inspected books" —work that was mostly looking at pictures in new books. Mr Harris taught Betty and Pamela how to put pockets on the back flap of the book for the check-out cards that he was typing. Betty had been making book spine labels after Mr Harris handed her the check-out card. Pamela made sure that the label got on the right book and that the card matched the book.

Mr Harris insisted that he would stock the wood stove. Josephine explained that she could carry firewood, but he said, "I understand, my dear Miss Josephine, but I want to take care of my little library ladies." Josephine could not fight Mr Harris and all his spoiling.

Each afternoon, Mr Harris would stop their work for a "little rest" from library chores. Sitting in his rocking chair, with his hands on his broad little belly, his eyes twinkling behind the round glasses, Mr Harris read stories. He was a wonderful storyteller and would stop reading, look up from the book, adjust his little round glasses, and smile. He gave them just enough time to wonder how any Little Rabbit or Jack the Trickster would ever get out of this fix. Then he would clear his throat and continue until Little Rabbit or Jack was home around the fire with a great story to tell.

Josephine loved storytellers and was determined to be one—just like Mother. After Mr Harris read a new story, she would practice it by telling it to herself. When she really knew it, she would tell it to Nora Ann.

Nora Ann loved to sneak into Josephine's bed when the lights in the cottage were out and listen to stories. When Nora Ann and Josephine were snuggled together, it almost felt as if Mother was in the room with them. Nora Ann's favorite snuggle up story was the story of why Brother Possum loves peace. Josephine had thought this was because of the tickling at the end of the story—until last night.

As Nora Ann and Josephine snuggled in bed, Josephine decided to do a let's-go-to-sleep version of Brother Possum. She would tell an abbreviated story, tickle Nora Ann, who was Brother Possum, and they would go to sleep. She began her story…

Brother Possum Loves Peace

Possum and Raccoon were walking along and having a nice little confab. Suddenly along comes Bad Dog who was just raring for a fight. "Are you with me Possum?" asked Raccoon just as Bad Dog attacked.

As soon as Dog jumped Possum, Possum fell on the ground like he was dead. Laid there just as stiff as a board and didn't wiggle a finger or a nose. Raccoon was a great fighter and soon Dog knew he was beat. As soon as Raccoon let loose, that Dog ran away with his tail between his legs. No more fighting. Raccoon looked at Possum just lying stiff on the ground, turned up his nose, and walked on home.

Later that week, when Raccoon and Possum met on the road, Possum asked if Raccoon wanted to come for some dinner. Raccoon said he didn't have dinner with no cowards. He said he would not be friends with anyone that wouldn't join him in a fight. "I don't need anybody with me that just lays down and plays dead at the first sign of trouble," he snarled.

Then Possum began to laugh. "You thought that I was scared? Well, not so, my friend. I could have taken that dog down all by myself. I knew you could as well.

But before I could begin to fight, that old Dog sniffed my ribs and all my tickle bones jumped. I just froze up with all the ticklin' on my ribs. Guess it looked like I was dead, but I was just tickled to death for a little while."

Raccoon looked at his friend and raised up an eyebrow. Possum said, "Just know that if you want someone with you, it will have to be in a fight with no ticklin' allowed." The End

Josephine giggled, "And now you know what comes next, Nora Ann? It's the tickling!"

She started to tickle Nora Ann who stiffened up, closed her eyes, and held her breath. She was playing dead, just like Possum, Josephine realized. "Nora Ann, you are so smart. You are acting out the story. You are Possum for sure!"

Nora Ann opened her eyes. "I'm not Possum. I'm Mother. I am only playing dead. I will wake up and get my girls. We can go home," sighed Nora Ann as she stiffened up and shut her eyes.

Josephine froze and then her eyes filled with tears. She had no words to explain that life was not like a story, and that their mother was not like Possum and just playing dead. "Nora Ann," she whispered, "do you really think that Mother is alive?"

Nora Ann kept her eyes closed and lay stiff. "Nora Ann?" she said again. A minute passed as Nora Ann held her breath and didn't move.

Finally, Nora Ann opened one eye. "What?" she said.

"Do you really think Mother is still alive?" Josephine repeated.

"Maybe," said Nora Ann squinting, "maybe, maybe, maybe. I wish, I wish, I wish, I might, have my mother dear tonight…"

Josephine snuggled closer until she felt Nora Ann relax and snuggle back. "You know what Daddy always said about wishes…" she said.

A moment passed and they said in unison, "If wishes were horses, beggars would ride!" Nora Ann sighed and put her arms around her big sister.

"We don't have our mother. We have each other," Josephine whispered.

Appalachian Jackson Orphanage
December 1919

As Christmas Day got closer, Nora Ann declared that Mr Harris was really St. Nicholas. Josephine agreed that Mr Harris looked a lot like Saint Nicholas with his glasses and round stomach and merry smile. Josephine asked Nora Ann where Mr Harris hid his beard, red suit and hat. Nora Ann said that Mr. Harris had a "Secret Santa Door" in the library.

The only Christmas stories their mother ever told were about the baby in the manger, the angels and the three kings. Then one year, mother read a poem, *A Visit from St. Nicholas*. Josephine asked for the poem again and again until she knew it by heart. She told it to Nora Ann every night before they went to bed.

Three days before Christmas, as the Duke sisters went to the library for work, Nora Ann could not stop talking about St. Nicholas. As soon as she saw Mr Harris standing in the library doorway, she began to run, yelling, "Mr Harris, where is St. Nicholas? Where are his reindeer?"

Josephine ran after her, but Nora Ann got in the door first and headed straight to Mr Harris who was unwrapping a new book. Mr Harris opened the book and read aloud as Nora Ann jumped up and down when she saw St. Nicholas on the book cover. *T'was the Night Before Christmas* is based on the poem *Visit from St. Nicholas* by Clement Moore, illustrated by Jessie Wilcox Smith."

When Josephine realized it was Mother's poem, she began to recite, "T'was the night before Christmas, when all through the house, not a creature was stirring, not even a mouse…" Mr Harris joined in as Nora Ann danced around the room, "The stockings were hung by the chimney with care, in hopes that St. Nicholas soon would be there…"

Nora Ann grabbed Mr Harris's coat sleeve and demanded, "Please show us the pictures. Josephine tells me the story every night. Pleeeese, Mr Harris." As Mr Harris read, Josephine was lost in the illustrations and his voice. Sometimes she imagined her mother's voice whispering with Mr Harris. Maybe Christmas—even at the orphanage—would have some surprises.

***

On Christmas Eve, Josephine could not stop thinking about their Christmases at home in the mountains. They had a tree, lots of singing and Mother's stories when they came home from church. Nora Ann had moved into Josephine's bed and was already asleep. Josephine was lulled to sleep by Nora Ann's breathing and memories of her mother's smile as she tucked them into bed on Christmas Eve.

They had only been asleep for a few hours, when Nora Ann bolted up in bed and whispered, "Do you hear that…the prancing and pawing of each little hoof?" Josephine was awake in a minute. Nora Ann was right. There was noise in the cottage even though the lights were out.

She put her finger to her lips to silence Nora Ann. Josephine waited for her eyes to adjust to the darkness. Then she saw someone with a round little belly and a sack on his back. There was a slight glow from the wood stove. Josephine saw and smelled a small pine tree in the corner of the cottage. The stranger was taking out wrapped boxes and putting them near the little tree.

Josephine waited for the poem's "wink of his eye and a nod of his head" but this didn't happen. The cottage door silently closed, and all was quiet again. Josephine hugged Nora Ann and whispered that it was St. Nicholas, but they had to wait until morning to see the tree and presents. "Same rules that we had at home," she reminded the excited Nora Ann.

In the morning, they awoke to the smallest pine tree decorated with only a straw star on the top and paper stars. It smelled just like Christmas and under the tree was a gift for everyone in the cottage. Betty got a beautiful blue sweater with matching socks. Pamela got a book by Annette Kellerman, *How to Swim*. Nora Ann got a soft teddy bear. Josephine could tell by the package that her gift was a book. She slowly opened it and found a book of poems, *A Child's Garden of Verses* illustrated by Jessie Wilcox Smith. One picture was of little girls reading a book on a window seat in a fancy house. Josephine wondered if the Stevenses were working with St. Nicholas. They had pancakes for breakfast and sang Christmas carols after lunch and dinner. Josephine admitted that it did seem a lot like Christmas.

Chapter 11: The Old South

King Ferry New York
June 2019

My family would go south every summer to visit my Aunt Nora and her family in Florida. We would leave while it was still dark. My brother and I would immediately fall asleep until we were halfway through Virginia.

As a teenager, I noticed something unusual about my mother's voice as we traveled south. She would begin to drawl as soon as we reached North Carolina. Words that were crisp and sharp like "green" in Maryland would lull into two syllables "grrrr-eeen" in North Carolina.

I never thought of my mother as a Southerner. She was liberal in so many ways. She stood with her hero Eleanor Roosevelt in freedom and equality for all people regardless of gender, race or economic class. Mother did not conjure the "South" except in story, and the lilt of her southern accent.

Mr Harris and his stories would always be with Josephine in a library. Like Josephine, Mr Harris had been shaped by the South, but not limited. He knew that iron had both color and endless shapes. Mr Harris used books to present many sides of any issue. He had shaped her thinking forever on the Civil War.

When Josephine and her college roommate, Elaine Greer, had traveled to Warrenton, North Carolina, to see other college friends, they had stopped at the Annie Carter Lee Monument. Annie, the daughter of General Robert E. Lee, died in October of 1865 in Sulphur Springs, Warren County, North Carolina.

Standing in front of the obelisk grave marker, Josephine envisioned Mr Harris with a biography of Robert E. Lee in his hand and passion in his voice, "General Lee could not bury his daughter in the family cemetery because it would involve moving her body over Union lines. It would be five years before General Lee could even visit his daughter's grave.

"Both Abraham Lincoln and Robert E. Lee lost beloved children during the Civil War and could not leave their battle posts. On the day the Civil War ended with Lee's surrender at Appomattox, President Lincoln set a holy example of dignity and forgiveness. When

General Lee surrendered to General Grant, Lincoln admonished the country to 'judge not that we be not judged.'

"Lincoln ended by calling for a day of national thanksgiving. 'He, from whom all blessings flow, must not be forgotten,' he said. It was his last speech before he was assassinated by John Wilkes Booth.

"President Lincoln wanted to bring the nation together. He saw reconstruction as a time of both healing and justice for those who had been enslaved, ravaged by the war, or isolated by regional history. He knew we were a great nation, and, with time, we would become even greater."

In her imagination, Josephine saw Mr Harris holding up another book—a copy of Samuel Smith's *"Hero Series, Abraham Lincoln"*. Mr Harris had introduced the book, written in 1902, by reading Smith's essay establishing Lincoln as one of the few authentic American heroes. The book ended with *Words of Lincoln*. Mr Harris challenged the students, "I will give special credit to any students who can quote Lincoln."

Josephine read the book and began to memorize. Her favorite Lincoln quote was, "My early history is perfectly characterized by a single line of Gray's *Elegy*: 'The short and simple annals of the poor.'"

Lincoln not only inspired Josephine, he made her smile. There was nothing wrong with being poor like Lincoln and nothing wrong with questioning some old-fashioned Southern ways.

Appalachia Jackson Orphanage
Winter 1920

Mr Harris was about to reveal a secret of his past. Like all Mr Harris' stories Josephine listened and memorized. As they huddled near the library stove, Mr Harris told about how he got a teaching job and then was dismissed. She wrote the story in a notebook that Mrs Stevens had given her. It was the only story Mr Harris ever told about himself. Josephine called it an iron story—reading it made you stronger.

Mr Harris' Tale of War and Truth

You will find Old South Preparatory for Young Confederate Men situated in one of the finest sections of Atlanta. My uncle explained that you could only be admitted if you were of the right lineage. You had to work hard, but hard work was not enough. You needed to be from a good family with a goodly amount of money.

The headmaster of the school valued family and money. My uncle did not tell me that the headmaster did not value change. Headmaster would never teach change because he believed the South was fine as it was. Let the Yankees have all the change they wanted.

The headmaster learned from my uncle that I came from wealth, family, and had graduated with honors from the University of Georgia. My uncle told him that I had just returned from service in the War to End All Wars and that I had been a specialist in code decryption and secret Allied communications. My uncle bragged, "His military record is exemplary and will be a great advantage for the school." I was hired on my uncle's recommendation alone.

What neither the headmaster nor my uncle knew was that war had reshaped me. While war did not make me a man—my family did that; war made me a different man. I now questioned, thought, and was not afraid to speak my mind. I could not wait to leave the battlefield for the classroom. I collected books for my young scholars, ideas for discussion, and writing challenges.

I cared for all those who had served the Allied Powers during the War—regardless of the color of their skin. Before my Army discharge, I learned about draft policies in the South that penalized my Georgia neighbors. Black men who owned their own farms and had families were often drafted before single white men

174

who worked on large plantations. Postal workers would not deliver registration cards of black men and worked with local sheriffs to have them arrested as draft dodgers. I wanted to make sure these policies would never occur again. The South had to change.

The headmaster required new teachers to submit their lectures for review. I was looking forward to discussing my "Let's Learn about the Army in the War to End All Wars" lecture when I was called into the headmaster's office. I took a seat and watched as the headmaster held up my lecture and dramatically ripped the pages into tiny pieces that snowed down on the oriental carpet in front of his ornate mahogany desk. Then he kicked the paper pieces with his highly polished leather shoes and finished by stomping them.

I watched this temper tantrum in silent amazement and listened as he ranted, "Your lecture disgusts me, Mr Harris. I insist on approving your lectures and any book that you recommend. You will never question our fine state of Georgia or mention Negro soldiers in this school again. Good Day!"

I smiled, stood up and methodically picked up every scrap of paper from the carpet and put them in my jacket pockets. Then I extended my hand to the headmaster. The headmaster was confused. A handshake meant agreement and he didn't know what he would be agreeing to. Still, he extended his hand.

As we stood shaking hands, I began, "Well, my dear headmaster, let's agree to disagree. If you want to approve of my every lesson and assigned book, I have one request. You must sit down with me, and we can discuss what you dislike about my work. If you can prove that my thinking is unscholarly, I will of course change my lessons and books."

The Headmaster's face grew redder and redder as he listened. He yanked back his hand from the handshake and roared, "Get out of my office, and out of our school! Go find a nice place up North for your disgusting ideas."

I continued to smile and stand my ground with my hand extended. After a minute, headmaster turned on his heel, stomped the floor, and left his office slamming the door. I waited until it was silent in the hallway, quietly opened the headmaster's office door and walked down the hallway of the preparatory for the last time.

As I packed up my desk, I remembered my favorite Professor of History at Georgia University whose motto was: "How little is the mind that is not open for discussion." I would find the school where I was meant to teach. The End

Chapter 12: The Three Pencilteers

Blue Ridge Summit Pennsylvania
October 1976

My mother, Josephine, sat with her grandson Timothy in her lap. They were both looking out the window at the trees beginning to change color and the steep fall from the edge of the house down the path to the road. My five-year-old son snuggled closer to my mother and asked, "Grandma, what would happen if the house started to fall down the mountain?" After the slightest pause, my mother began...

One day Timothy and his grandmother were sitting in the house that belonged to his grandparents. Gramma had just given Timothy a warm oatmeal raisin cookie when they heard a noise. "What was that?" asked Timothy in a funny I-have-a-mouthful-of cookie voice.

His gramma took him in her arms when they felt the house begin to slide. Gramma said something about Iron Pants as they flew out the front door and watched the house begin to slide down the hill toward the road.

The house bumped and thumped against rocks and trees. When it hit the road, it stopped and wobbled on the edge of the mountain and the valley far below. Timothy and his Gramma ran down the path to the road. Grampa came running after them. He had a big rope in his hands.

Grampa curled the rope like a lasso and threw it around the chimney of the house just in time. Timothy, Gramma and Grampa pulled and then tied the rope around a huge oak tree that was over 150 years old. The house stopped wobbling. Grampa smiled and then they all laughed.

"Well," said Grampa, "I guess we better start walking this house back up the hill brick by brick. We can do it before the first car comes down the road if we work hard."

They were very hard workers. The house was back on its foundation before they knew it. And the most wonderful part was, when they went into the kitchen the oatmeal cookies were still warm. The End

My son looked at his grandmother and said, "Tell it again, Gramma. Please! And who is Iron Pants?"

Whenever Mother told a story, I always imagined her two best friends from the orphanage, Walter and Virginia, sitting in the room. Walter would be taking notes and Virginia would be drawing. Mr Harris had named them the Three Pencilteers.

Another semester was beginning. It was hard for Josephine to believe that she had been at Appalachian for almost a year. There were two new cottages opening and twenty-four new students would be arriving this week. Josephine wasn't sure if any of the new students would be in her class. She had been in fifth grade since September and still didn't have a real friend yet. She spent her time with her sisters and with Mr Harris in the library. She hoped her classmates didn't think she was unfriendly, but that they realized she was just shy.

Josephine envied all the friends Pamela was making on the swim team. She watched Pamela practice in the new swimming pool and listened as the coach told them how to improve as individual swimmers and as a team. They were beginning to learn who had speed and who had endurance.

One evening before chapel, Josephine told her sisters that she might want to try out for the team. Nora Ann piped up, "Me, too."

Pamela stood up, put her hands on her hips and using her best Coach Jensen voice told them she would teach them how to improve their starting position. "Josephine, Nora Ann stand here." They stood at the end of the rug in the cottage and pretended they were getting ready to jump into the pool at the beginning of a race.

Pamela's Coach Jensen voice improved as she lectured, "On the block, your 'take-your-mark' position primes you for action. Four things to be mindful of:

1. High Hips
2. Eyes Looking Down
3. Arms Loaded
4. Rear Foot Behind Your Hips"

As Josephine and Nora Ann tried to keep their hips high, eyes down, arms strong and rear foot back, Pamela scolded. "No, Josephine, keep your arms strong. Look, I can just push them, and you are unbalanced. Tense those muscles!" She pushed Josephine's arms again and again, harder each time.

"Nora Ann! Hips high!" Pamela went behind Nora Ann and grabbed her hips and began to lift them. When she lifted Nora Ann's hips, Nora Ann raised her feet and balanced on one hand. She looked like a bird on the wing.

Josephine was glad that she didn't have her eyes down. Nora Ann yelled, "I'm a bird, not a fish!" Josephine was amazed at how strong she was to balance on one arm.

Pamela was surprised, but not delighted. "Nora Ann, put down your arm. I am letting go of your hips. Now!"

"No! I want to fly, and you need to hold me up until I figure out how to flap my wings and take off," Nora Ann yelled.

Josephine joined the spirit of rebellion, "Pamela, lift me up so I can try and fly," she laughed.

"I am counting to three and I am letting go of you, Nora Ann. Josephine, you better come here to catch this little bird that is about to fall out of the nest. You can learn to fly together and forget the swim team. You are both hopeless! One, two, two-and-a-half, three!"

Josephine was there just in time to block Nora Ann's fall. Pamela almost walked over them both as she stomped toward the door. At the doorway, she looked over her shoulder and hissed, "Birds of a feather flock together."

Miss Faircloth's voice startled them, "Sisters…" She was standing behind Pamela in the open door. "I am very proud that you are both fish and fowl and I am especially glad that Pamela is on our swim team." She gave Pamela a little pat on the shoulder and said, "I think it might be getting time for chapel. I will bring these little birds along. Catch up to Betty." Pamela smiled at Miss Faircloth and gave her younger sisters a you-are-hopeless look as she left.

Miss Faircloth picked up Nora Ann and told her to get a sweater before they left. Then she turned to Josephine and said that she had a special spot for her in chapel. She explained that two new fifth-grade students had arrived and were staying with Doctor and Mrs Wesler until the new boys' cottage was ready in two days. "I think it would be good for you all to get to know each other."

Josephine wondered if she wanted Miss Faircloth choosing her friends but replied in what she hoped was a polite voice, "I would love to meet the new students. It will be nice not to be the newest student in our class."

Nora Ann returned with a threadbare brown sweater and a red sweater with missing buttons. Miss Faircloth surveyed the worn sweaters, "I think the red sweater is more cheerful." Nora Ann dropped the brown sweater and was still putting the red one on when Miss Faircloth urged, "Let's go girls. Nora Ann, it is time for Josephine to meet some new friends."

"Okay," said Nora Ann. "Remember, Josephine, at the beginning of the race there are four rules: Wiggle your hips, roll your eyes, load up your arms and keep your rear near your foot." Miss Faircloth and Josephine laughed out loud. When Miss Faircloth did a sort of combination snort and laugh, Josephine laughed even harder.

***

The two new students were standing where Doctor Wesler had left them—in the front of the chapel by the first pew. Josephine could tell how uncomfortable the boy and girl were. It did seem that everyone was looking right at them, and for good reason. The girl was almost a foot taller than the boy and had long red curls. Josephine guessed she wouldn't get her haircut until she moved into the cottage. She was wearing one of the orphanage's ragged dresses, but the faded green of the dress matched her eyes. She stood close to the boy. When she wasn't looking down, she was looking at the boy.

Even though he was short, the boy seemed like the stronger of the two. He had his feet planted slightly apart, his hands were in fists, and he was not wearing old clothes, but a nice white shirt that fit and pants that did not have patches. His brown hair was parted and combed to the side and his green eyes had little flecks of gold in them. He was looking at the girl, and then he scanned the children in the pews as if daring anyone to get in his way. Josephine wondered how they knew each other and why they were at the orphanage.

Miss Faircloth lightly took Josephine's arm and pushed her to the front of the chapel. "Josephine, I would like to introduce you to two of your classmates,

183

Virginia Dare White and Walter Raleigh Duke. Walter, Josephine's last name is Duke also."

Virginia looked up and gave Josephine a shy smile. Walter unclenched his fists and said, "Where are you from, Miss Duke?"

"Why Mr Walter Raleigh Duke, I am from the dirt-poor region of the Warren County Appalachian Mountains. As I was taught to say, 'I am a poor Duke, not a Biddle Duke.' Where are you from, Sir Walter—England?"

Miss Faircloth gasped. Walter put out his hand as he stifled a laugh. "Pleased to meet you, Miss Duke. I am not from England, and I look forward to discussing which one of us is poorer very soon. Have you met my friend Virginia Dare? She is a very famous woman, being the first English child born and baptized in America. Sadly, the location of her birth was the lost colony of Roanoke. We can discuss heritage, poverty and losing a colony when we have more time."

Virginia nodded at Josephine. Miss Faircloth looked like she wanted to forget all introductions and find another job. Suddenly the piano began to play *Onward Christian Soldiers*. Miss Faircloth shoved them into the first pew and handed them hymnals. "Let's forget the talking and just sing. Please!"

When the hymn was over, they sat down. Josephine, Walter and Virginia all kept their eyes down, like they were about to begin a swim meet at the starting line. Josephine wondered if she was at the beginning of a new race—with a team of new friends. Josephine was thinking about a new team, when Doctor Wesler proclaimed, "Our Bible reading this evening is from the book of Revelations:

I am Alpha and Omega, the beginning and the ending, saith the Lord, which is, and which was, and which is to come, the Almighty."

Josephine watched Virginia. She had nervous hands and played with an old white handkerchief that had a pretty crocheted edge of lavender thread. Josephine wondered who gave her the handkerchief and who had done the crocheting. She wondered if she was thinking about these people as she twisted the cloth and ran her fingers along the lavender stiches. Josephine wanted to know her story and why someone called her Virginia Dare; what had they hoped to accomplish giving someone a name that everyone associated with a lost colony and a woman that was changed into a white doe? A deer not bread dough.

Walter Raleigh only had his eyes down for a moment before his gaze moved to the chapel window. He was not paying attention to a word that was being said, or at least that was the impression he gave with his faraway eyes and slack shoulders. He was no longer the feisty warrior, but more a day-dreamy poet. Josephine liked the idea of having a friend who was a warrior and a poet.

Josephine's own daydreaming ended when she heard hymnals being opened and Doctor Wesler announcing the closing hymn. She decided to sing softy and listen to see if Virginia and Walter could carry a tune. Virginia had a lovely clear soprano voice and sang like she knew the hymn very well and had sung it frequently. Walter still had a high voice that occasionally would crack and be low. He sang loud for someone who was mostly making up the music and reading the words. The song ended and everyone began to move out of the pews.

"We have to wait for Doctor Wesler," said Virginia. "Can you wait with us Josephine?"

Josephine looked at Miss Faircloth who nodded yes. "Have the Weslers walk you back to our cottage. It is right on the way to their house. I'll go find Nora Ann."

Soon they were the only three people left in the pews. Doctor Wesler had gone to the back of the altar and was talking to Mrs Wesler and the pianist.

"Well, it is safe to say that we are all here because our parents have died," said Walter. "I wonder if we could just not talk about this tonight. Maybe you girls want to talk about this, but I can't stand it any more."

"I agree, Walter. Josephine and I can talk about whatever we want when you are not around." Virginia looked at Josephine who smiled. Virginia talked as if they were already friends. Just as quickly, Virginia lowered her eyes and looked painfully shy. "That was presumptuous of me, Josephine. You can talk to anyone you want."

"I want to talk to you, Virginia. And I want to introduce you both to my sisters, but not tonight." She saw Virginia's face relax and they both looked at Walter.

"Well, I guess it's up to me to talk, since I told everyone what they couldn't talk about," said Walter. He almost sounded apologetic, but not quite. "I know, we can talk about the sermon. Do you think Alpha is a girl's name and Omega is a boy's name? If you had twins and one was a girl and one a boy, would you name them Alpha and Omega?"

Josephine could hardly believe her next words, "Well, Walter, the pressure to be godly on these little ones would be very great. I don't think I would want one to think they were always first in line and the other one to think they had to be last. I think it is a bad idea, Walter. What do you think?"

"Well, if I had twins and one was a boy and the other a girl, I would name them Walter and Virginia and I would leave off the Raleigh and Dare. They could be best friends and get through anything and not have to be too godly. What do you think, Virginia?"

Virginia was the most relaxed Josephine had seen her and she smiled at Walter. "Yes, I like the names for your twins, Walter. Josephine, what would you name twins?"

"I too would have a boy and girl. I would name one after my mother Patti and one for my favorite boy's name Carl. Do you think they would have a twins' club and the girls would play with each other and Carl and Walter would be friends?"

They heard the door close, and Doctor Wesler walking up behind them. Walter winked and said in a slightly louder voice, "I agree, ladies, that Alpha and Omega are powerful ideas and that tonight's sermon was exceptional."

He turned around and acted surprised to see Doctor Wesler. Virginia and Josephine lowered their eyes and tried not to smile. "Doctor Wesler, we have to escort Miss Josephine Duke to her cottage, and I know it has been raining. I forgot my cloak. Can I borrow your jacket if we come to any puddles?"

Doctor Wesler did something Josephine had never seen him do. He slapped Walter on the back and laughed. "Well, Sir Walter Raleigh, I am glad you are living up to your name. Sadly, I only have one good jacket, so tonight we are going to avoid puddles. Is that okay with you, girls?"

"Yes, sir," Virginia and Josephine said in unison. They looked at each other and laughed. Doctor Wesler made sure Josephine got to her cottage. As he turned to leave, Walter said in a loud voice, "See you at lunch tomorrow, Josephine." Virginia smiled and blew a kiss. Josephine could hardly wait for lunch the next day.

***

After breakfast, Betty, Pamela and Josephine went to the library to work. Mr Harris asked Betty and Pamela to help him create a display of books for high school students. Pamela selected two books about swimming and Betty had a book on the life of Clara Barton, the famous nurse. There was a newly opened box that Mr Harris said had just arrived from the Stevenses—all biographies. Betty selected a book about Abraham Lincoln and put it next to Clara Barton.

Josephine picked up the Lincoln book and just flipped to a page. As her eyes scanned the words, she read, "It was at the time of his mother's death that the sadness that never left him came upon him." Her eyes filled with tears, and she was about to put the book back, when Betty was at her side. "That book was in the wrong box. It really goes with the books in a series that you have about children's heroes."

Josephine took the book and put in on the table by a sign that said, Fifth and Sixth Grade Favorites. She decided to make a display of children's heroes and began to take all the books out of the box. She could not believe her eyes when the first book she withdrew was *Children's Heroes Series: The Story of Sir Walter Raleigh* by Margaret Duncan Kelly. She held the book in her hands and was drawn into the cover illustration. Sir Walter had a neatly trimmed beard, a high forehead and dark eyes that stared right at you. He had a fancy hat with red ribbons and jewels, a white ruff collar and his famous red cloak—ready for any lady (or queen!) in distress.

Josephine began to unpack the books from the box of children's heroes. She noticed something unusual about the books...Abraham Lincoln, Walter Raleigh, David Livingstone, Captain Cook, and then Lord Nelson and Sir Francis Drake.

Mr Harris came over to where Josephine was working. "How do you like the new series of heroes?"

"They are beautiful books. Are heroes only boys?"

Mr Harris looked startled and then pensive. "As always, an excellent observation, Josephine. Let's keep looking." He pulled out Lord Clive, Columbus,

Napoleon and then to Mr Harris' great relief the story of Joan of Arc. One of nineteen books was about a girl.

Mr Harris smiled and handed Josephine the book. The cover had Joan holding a huge staff with a white flag covered with golden fleur-de-lis. She was surrounded by armored soldiers brandishing swords and was clearly leading the charge. Josephine tried to smile back while she replied, "Is the definition of a hero someone who does battle, leads an army, and conquers weaker nations? I guess that is why we only have Joan of Arc. I wonder how the head of your school in Atlanta would answer this question. I bet he would be all for war."

Mr Harris nodded. "We need books about heroes that do more than lead us into battles." He went to his desk and got a pen and sheet of paper. "I need the Duke sisters here immediately. Let's make a list of all the girls and women we want to know about, and I will try to find books about them."

"I want to know more about Virginia Dare and famous women writers and illustrators," Josephine declared. Betty added famous nurses and doctors to the list. Pamela added women swimmers and film stars to the list.

Mr Harris was writing furiously. "You are the best library helpers in all of North Carolina. What would I do without the Duke sisters?"

Their conversation was interrupted by arrival of Miss Faircloth followed by Walter and Virginia. Walter was holding a box. Virginia's eyes scanned the room and she smiled when she saw Josephine standing near the table of books.

Josephine walked over to them, took Virginia's hand and gave her a smile. Walter joined them and put the box of books he was carrying on the table. "Mr Harris," said Walter, "these books belonged to my family, and I wondered if you would want any in our library."

Mr Harris walked over to Walter and smiled while he patted him on the shoulder. "Let's have a look, Sir Walter."

Mr Harris helped Walter unpack the box of books. The first books to come out of the box were adventure books for boys and girls—*Rover Boys*, *Motor Boys*, *Patty Fairfield* and *Marjorie Maynard* series. Then Mr Harris pulled out the *Bobbsey Twins* with the picture of Freddie and Flossie on the cover. Freddie was holding a buttercup under Flossie's chin to see if she liked butter.

"My little sisters and I loved the buttercup test," sighed Mr Harris.

"My twin sister and I loved to do this, too," said Walter.

No one said a word as Walter and Mr Harris kept taking out books. "I think this is all of the children's books," said Walter. "The rest were my father's, but I think someone would still like to read them."

Walter pulled out a worn black leather book with gold lettering—*Navigation and Nautical Astronomy* by Coffin. "It's sort of funny. My father had two copies of this book—one belonged to his father. My grandmother put the older copy of this in my father's coffin. 'Coffin in the coffin' as we like to say."

Mr Harris watched Walter remove the rest of the books. "Well, Walter, you have contributed richly to our library. Just looking at these books reminds me of all the books I yet haven't read. Sometimes this makes me happy and sometimes I just look at the books and feel tired. Let's take a break and walk over to the swimming pool. I want Miss Pamela to tell us all about what she is learning about being our next Elaine Golding, the first woman to swim part of the Panama Canal."

Pamela stopped writing library cards, threw down her pen, picked up the article Mr Harris had found about Elaine Golding, and assumed leadership of the group. They walked across the grounds from the library to the pool.

Pamela opened the door to the new building and walked immediately to the edge of the pool. She straightened up, her face relaxed into a smile, and she asked, "What do you want to know about swimming and our new swim coach and teams?"

Virginia was the first to speak, "Who is the swim coach and are the teams only for high school?"

"Thanks, Virginia. Sadly, the only teams we have right now are high school teams, but that might change when our new coach arrives. Coach Jensen is from Asheville. She has recently returned from New York where she made it to the final cut for the 1920 Women's Swim Team for U.S. summer Olympics in Antwerp, Belgium. I believe she has some ideas for swimsuits that will allow our women swimmers to have a new competitive advantage."

Mr Harris encouraged them to walk around the pool and ask any other questions. Walter climbed the ladder and stood on the diving board. He seemed very comfortable around the pool Josephine thought. She would tell Walter about Nora Ann's new rules for starting positions. Mr Harris looked at his pocket watch and announced it was time to head to the dining hall for lunch.

Walter, Virginia and Josephine were the first outdoors. Josephine asked Virginia if she wanted to try out for the swim team if the new coach created one. "No, I was just curious. I know that Walter and his sister were great swimmers before his family got sick and his father went overseas for World War I." Josephine looked at Walter who gave Virginia a little smile and walked faster.

Josephine grabbed Virginia's hand and walked to catch up with Walter. "You know that Pamela didn't learn to swim until she came to the orphanage. She was a natural and now wants to become a beautiful swimmer in moving pictures. What do you think about that, Walter?"

Walter stopped suddenly and gulped like he was trying to swallow words or maybe his feelings. He closed his eyes for a minute and then he smiled his devilish grin and looked at Josephine. "Why, my dear Miss Duke, of course any Duke girl will accomplish whatever she sets her mind to doing…"

Then as suddenly as the smile appeared, it vanished, and Walter's eyes filled with tears. "Well, there was one exception, my dear sister Polly Amanda Duke wanted to be a scientist and was sure she would be the one to discover a cure for tuberculosis. She set her mind to it and fought a great fight, but tuberculosis won. Just as war took my father, tuberculosis took my mother and sister."

When they arrived at the dining hall, they ate lunch in silence.

***

Tuesday was the day for Virginia to get her hair cut with the famous bowl and scissors chop. By Saturday, Walter was furious. "Virginia, you know that your red curls remind me of my sister. I can't let this happen. At least we could save some curls and keep them in a box. Even if you don't have a mother or grandmother to care about the curls, I can care about them. We need a plan."

Josephine loved plans and was thinking how they could keep curls in a box. She was also remembering that her mother never saved any curls because her daughters always grew more. Walter said that his mother saved his sister's curls from her first haircut— but he didn't know where they had gone. He was determined not to lose any more red curls.

Josephine was obsessed with finding Walter a box for the curls. She was also concerned. "Walter, even if we could find a box, where would we hide it?" The girls had looked around their cottage and couldn't find anything.

Walter glanced at the clock. "We better be off to the library. We can't disappoint Mr Harris who will be waiting for his Saturday helpers. We can stop by the new boys' cottage on our way. The carpenters and painters have a few more touch ups before the cottage opens Monday. They might have a box lying around."

Walter had made friends with the carpenter who was supervising the building construction. When they arrived at the cottage, the carpenter greeted them, "Hi, Walter my lad, top of the morning." Walter shook hands with the carpenter while Virginia and Josephine stood by the door. The carpenter ushered them inside.

Josephine began to look around the room. Her eyes fell on an empty box of nails printed with the words, *Patent Wire Clinching Nails* and a drawing of two nails with the words Hold and Fast on either side. She picked up the box and took it over to Walter who was talking to the carpenter. Walter smiled, "Why Josephine, I can't believe you remembered that I needed a box. This is perfect." Then he looked at the carpenter. "I wanted to make sure our cottage stays sound—even after you and your men leave. I wonder if you could leave me a few nails and screws in case I need to repair something in the future. I am sure I could find a hammer and screwdriver, but not sure we would have nails as fine as yours."

"Walter my lad, you are always thinking. You will make a fine carpenter or teacher or preacher someday. I am sure you are the only boy to think of this. The box, nails and screws are yours! You are a man after my own heart." The carpenter patted Walter on the shoulder as he gave Walter nails and screws.

As they continued their walk to the library, Walter explained he could make a false bottom to the box that would neatly hold some lovely red curls. Mr Harris was waiting at the library door. Mr Harris smiled when Walter explained about the box of nails and screws and said that the new boys' cottage would be in capable hands. He didn't even ask Walter why he needed some cardboard to make a few improvements to the box as he outlined the library work for the morning.

***

It was easy for Walter to get some of Virginia's curls. He "unexpectedly" showed up at the girls' cottage on Monday just as the hair cut was finished. The curls were next to the stool where they had fallen.

Miss Faircloth had just taken the towel off Virginia's shoulders and was brushing her neck, when Walter knocked on the door. Using his most convincing Sir Walter gallantry, he politely offered to sweep up the curls and take them out for the birds, "My dear Miss Faircloth, Josephine has told me how you care for the birds and provide them with the softest materials for their nest building. May I take these outside and dispose of them by the dogwood trees? I think I saw some robins there yesterday when I was walking back from chapel."

"Why, Sir Walter Raleigh, you certainly are living up to your name. I would love your assistance. Perhaps Josephine can help you while Virginia and I finish up with her lovely haircut."

Walter was able to both smile at Miss Faircloth and turn slightly away as he grimaced at Virginia and

Josephine. Josephine got the dustpan and broom from the closet and Walter swept up curls.

They made three trips because of all the hair. Walter chose the best curl from each dustpan and stuck them carefully in his pocket. "I will be able to slip these curls in the nail box before the other boys arrive after lunch. I can't wait to meet the other fellows in our new cottage."

When Walter and Josephine returned, Virginia was running her fingers through her short hair. Walter waved his box in the air, "I want to tell the story of how we stole these curls. Maybe we could make a book."

The Three Pencilteers ran by the pile of curls that the robins had already discovered. Virginia laughed and said, "If we made a book, I know what the cover would be. I can't wait to draw a robin's nest dripping with red curls."

Appalachian Jackson Orphanage
Fall 1920

Walter, Virginia and Josephine had been working together through the spring and summer and sixth grade was about to begin. Mr Harris had read them two books and told countless stories. They had created book displays for summer reading and were working on a display Walter wanted to call *What to Read When you*

Don't Want to do Homework. Mr Harris had been busy in Doctor Wesler's office and would return for their break.

As always, they had been trying to guess what Mr Harris might read, and they were perplexed when Mr Harris returned. He didn't have a book, but a box that he emptied on the library table. There was drawing paper, three pens, pencils and one set of watercolors. "I was thinking of you as my Three Musketeers and had a copy of Alexandre Dumas' book ready to read for our break. But when I looked at the cover and saw the brandished swords, I heard another voice saying, "The pen—"

"Is mightier than the sword," shouted Josephine, Walter and Virginia.

They looked at each other and then at Mr Harris. Virginia grabbed a pen and piece of paper. On the top she wrote The Three Pencilteers. Mr Harris laughed and then watched as Virginia's pencil created a very recognizable Walter, Josephine and Virginia brandishing pencils like swords.

Walter smiled as Virginia drew. "Well, Josephine, we need to write a story for our accomplished illustrator. Any ideas on how it will begin?"

Josephine smiled and began:

One fine day, Brer Harris decided to build a library, but he didn't have any books. He looked high and low and there were no books to be found. "Guess I will have to write some books of my own," he said scratching his head with his rear paw. "But what should I write about?"

Virginia had already begun to draw Brer Harris—a combination of a rabbit and Mr Harris. Walter and Josephine took up the tale. It was a story they had been working on since Walter had collected Virginia's red curls after her orphanage haircut.

Mr Harris left, and Walter wrote down the words to the story. Virginia continued with the pictures. Miss Fancy Dress looked so much like Miss Faircloth and Walter's fancy britches shown like polished metal. "How did you learn to draw?" Josephine asked.

"From my aunt, she was a book illustrator for St. Nicholas Magazine before she died—the first one we lost to good ole' tuberculosis. We should have our group of Pencilteers take on Mr Tuberculosis. I could destroy him over and over with my sharp pencils and drown him in watercolors."

Mr Harris gave the Pencilteers the time needed to finish their story. Virginia's illustrations inspired Walter and Josephine. The cover of the finished book was a robin's nest made with red curls, mud, straw and grass. Walter began the completed story in his most dramatic voice. Josephine and Virginia read the parts of the Little Girl Rabbits in perfect unison as Mr Harris listened.

Brer Walter and the Ruby Reds

Once there was a very tricky boy rabbit with a magic box. This box was not what it seemed to be. "I have my eyes on some treasure—some priceless ruby reds. When they hit the ground, I must be ready with a plan. I have my magic box, but who will help me steal my ruby reds?"

"Not so fast," said the Little Girl Rabbits. "You might be a tricky little fellow, but you forgot your enemy the wily Miss Fancy Dress. She will be watching you and guarding that treasure for her friends the little birds. She sure do fancy those little birds—more than any little boy bunny who is too big for his fancy britches."

Brer Walter snarled, "You don't talk about my fancy britches. They came from my rich, rich relatives and while they ain't 'round no more, these britches have special powers. I say these britches are a match for any ole dress ever made."

The Little Girl Rabbits smiled at him. Brer Walter stared back and said, "Yes, sir, I wonder if that Fancy

Dress and her birds think they deserve all the ruby reds? Well, they can think again. Wait until they turn their backs, and some of that treasure will be mine. I just need to lay low and watch. Yeah, just lay low and pounce when the time is right."

A door slammed, and the three rabbits turned to the cabin where Miss Fancy Dress and the girls slept. Through the cabin window they saw the flash of silver scissors. "Oh, here come the ruby reds. How are you going to steal them, Brer Walter? You can't just walk in there like a boy rabbit who forgot that only girls live in the Fancy Dress cabin."

Brer Walter laughed and rubbed his paws together. "The ruby reds will be mine and I will hide them right in plain sight—like the wily trickster I was born to be. I just need your help."

"We love adventures," said the Little Girl Rabbits in unison. The three approached the cabin and Little Girl Rabbits opened the door. Brer Walter was right behind them. "Miss Fancy Dress," they called, "Can we come in and bring our friend Brer Walter?"

Miss Fancy Dress frowned, but before she could speak, Brer Walter sang, "Brer Walter loves the little birds and wants to give them red ringlets. I am here with broom and bag to gather curls for nest-lets."

Before you could say Fancy Dress—the ruby reds were swept, the best secretly pocketed by Brer Walter *for his magic box, and the rest given to the birds. Brer Walter chuckled as he hid the box in plain sight in his cottage. He scorned those who missed what was right before their eyes. The End*

***

When Mr Harris asked how the second book was coming, Virginia answered in a solemn voice that she had already begun. Walter and Josephine stared at her in amazement. Virginia got her sketch book and opened it to an illustration. "I call this Thaddeus Beauregard Death—or T.B. for short," she explained. Mr Harris, Walter and Josephine stared at the picture of a ghost dressed in the finest clothes with a wide feathered hat, shining upraised sword, and with his leather-booted foot on a pile of dead animals.

"Wow," said Walter. "That is just the villain I want to defeat. We will have to get the wiliest of the animals for our story. I propose Sister Polly Amanda, an owl who studies everything about the ghost during her nighttime flights. She uses her wise owl science to make sure his killing will come to an end."

Josephine followed, "My animal is Mother Bear. She would do anything to keep Thaddeus Beauregard from her children. She is fierce! She throws logs and has claws that would rip his flesh. Wait, I guess a ghost doesn't have flesh. Walter, how does our story begin?"

Walter was about to speak when he saw Virginia looking at her sketch book with tears flowing down her cheeks. Josephine followed Walter's gaze and they quickly moved to either side of Virginia. "Virginia, we can write, and we can fight. But remember this is a villain we have all fought before and he has won," said Walter as he held Virginia's hand.

"Virginia, I think we feel stronger when we tell stories. We can use tricks and magic and one day that old Thaddeus Beauregard will be finished," whispered Josephine as she hugged Virginia. "Walter, please begin our story and I will jump in when I have an idea." Virginia grabbed her sketch book, and they finished the story that afternoon.

Thaddeus Beauregard and Mother Bear

Well, Brer Harris still was hankering for another book for his library. After he put the story of Brer Walter and the Ruby Reds on the shelf, he went searching for those three little storytelling rabbits.

He found them looking at a wanted poster with a horrific picture of a ghostlike nobleman with a big hat, fine clothes and a mighty sword. The name under the picture was "Thaddeus Beauregard—Reward $1,000."

"I could sure use a thousand dollars," said Brer Walter. "I could buy me some silver britches and then some gold britches for wearing to special occasions."

"Or we could bury you in those old britches," said the Little Girl Rabbits in one voice. "Nobody messes with old T.B. and wins."

Suddenly a soft whisper of wings and the appearance of a very sleepy little owl on Brer Walter's shoulder ended their conversation. The owl had a big leaf in her talons that she dropped when she began to whisper in Brer Walter's ear.

"I didn't know Brer Walter could understand Owl Talk," said the shortest of the girl rabbits.

"Me neither," said her taller sister. "I hope this is good news. I hope somebody has already captured old Thaddeus Beauregard and Brer Walter can live to tell another story."

The three rabbits commenced to scratch their ears when a great stomping sound came through the woods. Mother Bear started yelling as soon as she saw the rabbits, "Where is that thief? I don't make cornbread for it to be stolen while it is cooling on my window ledge." She was wearing a flour covered apron and had a wooden spoon in her hand that she was brandishing like ole T. B's sword. "Did you see a big fellow with a fancy hat and basket? He will wish he kept his thieving hands to himself when I catch up to him."

Brer Walter walked over to meet her with the leaf still in his hand. "Well, Mother Bear, just so happens I have information about that old thief. My little spy Polly Amanda Owl has seen this fellow and his basket. She says he is hiding in the woods and has his sword in its sheath."

"Be quiet, Mother Bear, and you might catch him sleeping," said the Little Girl Rabbits in unison. "He is very dangerous, and I wouldn't eat the cornbread if Mr T.B. had his hands on it," they warned.

Suddenly Polly Amanda Owl arrived with another leaf. She let the leaf fall on the ground in front of the group and flew off. Brer Walter picked it up and read: "Emergency, Thaddeus Beauregard is headed to the cabin with the little bear children. He has a basket in his hands. Mother Bear roars and takes off toward her cabin with the little rabbits following. They can't keep up with Mother Bear whose paws don't even seem to touch the ground.

When the little rabbits arrive at the cabin, they see Brer Mary running into the woods chasing Thaddeus Beauregard who still has the basket. "Nobody brings this stuff to my children. I'll catch you, you dirty thief and you will never mess with Mother Bear again."

The little rabbits wait with the little bears at the cabin for a week, but Mother Bear does not return.

Finally, Brer Walter hops down to the little Forest Folk Church in search of Brer Miller, the kindly deer who knows what to do when your mother doesn't come home. The End

As Walter softly read, "The End," Virginia began to cry. "Why do so many of our stories end this way. It's not fair. It's just not fair."

Josephine thought, "We need to plan our stories better. This was an honest story, but so sad. I don't think it has a moral. In fact, I am sure it does not have a moral."

Chapter 13: Creeds

King Ferry New York
October 2016

As I struggled to write my mother's story and create characters she might have known, a friend suggested that I write a creed for each character. I hoped she would not suggest that I begin by writing a creed for myself. I hated the thought of writing my own creed but loved the challenge of writing creeds for others. I would begin with a creed for my father.

I decided to write down all the statements of belief I remembered from my father over the years. I heard my father's voice with familiar clarity.

A man is as good as his word.

Use up, make do, and do without.

If that was my mess, I would clean it up.

Time to say goodnight young man, my daughter has lots of schoolwork to finish.

No son of mine is going to desert his duty.

When I don't know where I am as an old man, you can put me anywhere. For now, I want to stay in my own home.

My father didn't need a written creed. He lived his creed every day.

The last years of my mother's life, dementia clouded her thinking. She always knew the people around her and where she was, but her memory often failed. One morning in the last year of her life, my mother looked up from her breakfast plate and said to me, "Do you know what made your Father so special?" I shook my head and held my breath. "It was that he loved us so much. He just loved us."

Appalachian Jackson Orphanage
January 1921

Josephine was inspired. It seemed like a fun assignment—write your own creed. Her class had been studying the Apostle's Creed and had to memorize it for a test. Josephine was the first one called to recite. She thought for a moment that this was not fair. The last one to recite would have heard the words said twenty times. She was glad it was easy for her to memorize.

After everyone passed their recitation assignment, Josephine began writing her own creed. She played with a name she had secretly given herself. She would never turn in her Iron Pants Creed, but it was more fun to write than one about a sad little orphan girl. She could imagine Mr Barnes, her religion teacher, reading the Iron Pants Creed. Mr Barnes did not have a sense of humor, or as Doctor Stevens would have said, "The man lacks flexibility of thought." When she was finished, Josephine knew Iron Pants was a true creed, but one that Mr Barnes would never see.

The Iron Pants Creed

I, Josephine Helen Duke, believe that I will flourish and thrive because I know

THAT I will fight, and fight, and fight, and fight until my heart says STOP.

THAT I understand that I live in the South, but I am NOT the South as defined by know-nothings and other hicks.

THAT I will be careful of those who thump the Bible and respect those who live it.

THAT people can leave you and still love you very much.

THAT there are many ways of telling the truth, but I prefer to tell it using a story.

THAT singing is a way to lull you into change or accepting the hardest truths that you would not believe in a story.

THAT if you ever have to make a choice about people always stick with your family. They might not be perfect, but they are your family for a reason. Honor them.

THAT no one can put you down unless YOU let them. Being poor is not a disgrace, but a condition.

THAT education is the key to freedom.

THAT sometimes you need to use honey and not vinegar to get your way. I don't like this but have seen it to be true. Maybe I will just make them laugh instead of using honey.

Signed, Iron Pants, January 1921

When she finished, Josephine decided to write a creed for Betty, Pamela and Nora Ann. She took three pieces of paper and headed each one with a special name like her own Iron Pants.

The Gentle Shawl Creed

I, Betty Duke, *love my sisters because I was loved on this earth by our mother for the longest time. I was loved for fifteen years and because of this gift, I believe....*

212

The Silky Gloves Creed
I, Pamela Jane Duke, believe that sadness lives underneath my skin and seeps into my mind when I least expect it.

The Stubborn Mask Creed
I, Nora Ann Duke, believe that I will flourish and thrive because I know....

Josephine was startled when she realized it was time for breakfast. She quickly turned the papers over on her desk and left for the dining hall.

She didn't count on Nora Ann picking them up. Nora Ann arrived with the sheets of paper in her hand, crying, "It's the mailman... Rural Route Delivery for the Duke girls."

When Josephine saw the creeds, she grabbed the four papers out of Nora Ann's hand. Nora Ann immediately began to cry and then to wail. Betty scowled at Josephine. Pamela ignored her sisters and continued looking around the room for the swim team captain.

Miss Faircloth came over and picked up Nora Ann. "What is the matter, little mailman?"

"I had letters for all my sisters. Josephine wrote us all letters. One is long and three are very short. I thought I would deliver the mail, but Josephine grabbed them and now I have nothing for my Rural Route One delivery!"

Josephine regretted ever telling Nora Ann about the mail--- how it was delivered and asking her to say "Rural Route One" nine times fast.

She smiled at Miss Faircloth, "I am sorry, Miss Faircloth. I told Nora Ann that she could deliver mail and she got my homework by mistake. May I go to my room and get her the four sheets with our names on them—the mail that I wanted her to have?"

Nora Ann stopped wailing immediately. Josephine continued, "Maybe the mailman needs some extra butter for her pancake. I could give you my butter this morning, Mailman Nora Ann. Then we could play the say "Rural Route One" nine times fast game."

Nora Ann slowly smiled and hugged Miss Faircloth. "Say Rural Route One" fast for nine times— Go!" In a minute they were both tongue-tied and giggly.

Josephine backed away, "I'll go get the real mail. Be right back!" She was almost in the clear when she dropped two of the papers. Betty was there in a flash and picked them up. They were the ones titled Gentle Shawl and Iron Pants.

Betty read silently and then said, "I'll come with you to get Nora Ann's mail. We have to talk."

At the cottage Betty said, "Get four clean pieces of paper. I will help you address each one. We'll just write 'to' and our four names to save time. Then scribble on yours to make it look long. You promised Nora Ann four letters."

Josephine got the paper and two pencils, and, in a flash, they had four letters for Nora Ann.

Betty looked at the cottage door to make sure they were all alone, walked to Josephine and put her hand on her shoulder, "You are not allowed to name your sisters or define your sisters. The only one who can write a creed is the person themselves. You did a great job writing your creed and Iron Pants is a perfect name for you.

"But you never get to name or define your sisters. Do you understand? The people who were allowed to name us have died and we take their love to make our new lives. Do you understand me?"

Josephine put her hand on Betty's, "I am sorry, and you are right. I cannot name you or define you. I would like you to know that I gave you those names out of love." Her eyes began to fill with tears as she watched Betty's stern face.

At the sight of her sister's tears, Betty's eyes filled up. She whispered, "I know you love me. I love "Gentle Shawl" and your first sentence. I will write my own creed and when I am finished, I will share it with you—Iron Pants!"

They hugged and ran back to the cafeteria where Nora Ann took the new letters and happily delivered them to her sisters. Pamela looked at Betty. "You'd better tell me the whole story of these letters. I mean it!"

***

Betty worked on her creed for most of the week. When she finished, she called Pamela and Josephine together. She asked Josephine to read the Iron Pants creed for Pamela. Pamela laughed and said it fit Josephine perfectly.

Then it was Betty's turn to read her work. Josephine listened as Betty used "Gentle Shawl" as her name and repeated Josephine's first sentence. When she was finished, both Pamela and Josephine said in unison, "Read it again, please." Gentle Shawl smiled and read it again.

The Gentle Shawl Creed

I, Betty Duke, love my sisters because I was loved on this earth by our mother for the longest time. I was loved for fifteen years and because of this gift, I believe

THAT I will always think of my sisters first when any choice is offered.

THAT taking care of sisters is like taking care of anything; it takes time and patience.

THAT patience is quiet and gentle and does not give up.

THAT when you think that maybe it is time to think of only yourself, you remember your mother whispering, "You are my own big girl."

THAT losing patience is not a sin but only a shortcoming. Thank goodness for our Daddy laughing, "Well no one is perfect—but your mother is darn close. The reason I stick around is to serve as a bad example for you girls."

THAT taking care of yourself is also taking care of your sisters. This is an idea that was given to me by my favorite minister's wife to be.

THAT you can learn to take care of more people than just your sisters. Ministers, teachers, doctors and nurses are caregivers.

THAT education is necessary to learn to help those beyond your family.

THAT family teaches you about family.

THAT losing a mother does not make you a mother, no matter how hard you try.

Signed, Gentle Shawl, January 1921

Again, her sisters replied in unison, "Mother and Daddy are so proud."

Before they could speak again, Nora Ann came running into the room yelling, "Guess what? We are going to have cake. Doctor and Mrs Stevens have sent the whole school cakes—with icing! Chocolate! Vanilla! Strawberry! Come on before it's gone."

She ran toward the door and then turned around, "Guess what? Doctor and Mrs Stevens have finally adopted the four little boys that were living at the Reilly's house. Our Lazy Cat and her sister Daisy Cat now have four brothers. Praise the Lord and pass the cake!"

Pamela followed Nora Ann to the door. As Nora Ann ran ahead, Pamela put her arm around Josephine. "I like Silky Gloves and your first line. I will write my own creed, but don't want to share it. I want to keep on my silky gloves for now. For now, it will be cake and celebrating four lucky little boys."

"That's okay, Pamela. For now, cake and the Stevens' new family will be enough. Let's go eat."

Josephine was surprised to find Betty sitting on her bed crying the next evening. Josephine sat down by her and was silent. She saw that the paper on Betty's lap was Pamela's creed.

Betty took a handkerchief from her dress pocket and blew her nose. Then she patted Josephine's shoulder and folded the paper with Pamela's creed. "Someday Pamela will share this with you. I promised that I would let her do that. Is that okay, Iron Pants?"

218

Josephine nodded. "We are going to have to wait a long time for Nora Ann to write a creed. It will be worth the wait."

Chapter 14: In the Water

King Ferry New York
June 2014

As I write my mother's story, I am again torn by the stories of my Aunt Pamela and my brother Carl. They both carried a sadness that would change their lives. We now know so much more about mental illness, but so often then, and now, families struggle to help family members who are estranged by their health, poor choices and anger.

Pamela suffered the confines of a Southern marriage that separated her from her sisters and made it hard to raise her children as she wanted. Her depression grew and she was institutionalized by her family. My mother was not able to stay in touch with her sister. She did eventually find Pamela's sons and kept holiday cards and photos of what would have been Pamela's grandchildren.

Carl was drafted into the Vietnam War and came home changed. Not the way Mr Harris was changed but haunted by his experience. He spent years running from the war and finally with the help of loving people at the Paxton Street home he began to take the treatments he needed. He was able to declare, "I am tired of listening to the voices in my head. I am taking my medicine."

We never knew when Aunt Pamela stopped hearing voices or who helped her to end her sadness and pain. My mother bore her grief and relied on friends as well as family to cope.

Washington DC
August 1941

Josephine and Cleophas strolled down the streets looking at the shop windows. Fall clothes were on display. Cleophas joked that he had picked out his fall and winter clothes—or rather the Army had kindly done that for him.

As they sat down on a bench to watch the many soldiers and their dates walk by arm in arm, Cleophas again told Josephine how much he loved her letters, especially those with her stories about growing up in the orphanage. Her last letter had talked about the pool at the orphanage and Pamela's adventures.

Josephine moved closer as Cleophas put his arm around her. "Well, I am a Southern storyteller for sure. You are a good teller of tales yourself, but your style is very Northern. Why don't you tell me how you learned to swim? Tell it like a real storyteller."

Cleo laughed and without removing his arm from her shoulder began:

One day Cleo's older brother Dan threw him in the pond at their uncle's farm. The last words five-year-old Cleo heard were, "sink or swim," as he went under. As he struggled up for air doing a doggy paddle, he watched his brother Dan walk away. The End.

Josephine turned and she was almost in kissing reach of Cleophas' face. She tried to read his emotions as he continued. "I have always wondered if Dan's departure was a sign of faith in my swimming ability, or a desire for more dessert at the table. When I got to the edge of the pond, I ran after him and hit him as hard as I could. I think I knew he was really after an extra piece of cake, or that something was really bothering him. I guess he knew I was always Mother's favorite."

Appalachian Jackson Orphanage
Winter 1921

Nora Ann came running into the library. "Hurry up! We are having early dinner because of the swim meet. You

222

need to say grace, gulp food, and head for the pool. Pamela says to be ready for a big surprise."

Mr Harris opened the door for Nora Ann as she rushed out and urged them to follow her. Josephine, Walter and Virginia looked at Mr Harris. "I think you better do as Nora Ann says. I have heard a lot of rumors about tonight's swim meet."

When they got to the dining hall, they sat with Nora Ann as everyone bowed their heads. After grace, they grabbed their food and watched in amazement as Nora Ann's dinner disappeared before everyone's eyes. She was out the door, before they had barely finished their meal.

When they left the dining hall, they had to run to catch up to Nora Ann as she dashed toward the pool. As they entered the building, Josephine grabbed Nora Ann's hand. All the seniors in the girls' high school team were on the side of the pool, stretching and talking to Coach Jensen. They wore the standard swim dress with a fancy bodice, skirt and stockings.

"Where are the other girls? Where is Pamela?" Nora Ann whined. "I want a big surprise." As soon as the words were out of Nora Ann's mouth, she got her wish.

Running from the locker room, the rest of the girls' swim team joined the seniors. "They are wearing the boys' suits," whispered Nora Ann. The new girls' suits were a formfitting one piece with short sleeves, scooped necks and legs that ended mid-thigh.

"No, Nora Ann, they are a new style of suit. I think they might help Pamela and her teammates swim faster," whispered Josephine.

Josephine noticed that Pamela carried her favorite book *How to Swim.* She laid it on the bench before she joined the rest of the team and began stretching. The coach nodded to Pamela who picked up the book. She turned the pages to a bookmark and began to read as the girls' team and coach huddled around her.

"What is she reading?" asked Walter.

"It's the book she got for Christmas the first year we were here—Annette Kellerman's *How to Swim,*" Josephine answered.

Walter jumped up. "Annette Kellerman—Neptune's Daughter—Diving Venus—the inventor of the amazing form fitting swimsuit now known as *The* Annette Kellerman, the famous record-breaking, film star, lecturer for women's swimming and high diver herself? Josephine, you have to get me that book."

Coach Jensen clapped her hands. On command, the team sat on the benches by the pool. She nodded to Pamela and Ruth, a senior who was wearing the old uniform. Both girls went to the edge of the pool and took their starting positions.

As the starting gun sounded, Pamela hit the water, and immediately took the lead. The girls were doing the breaststroke. The coach ran to the other end of the pool with a stopwatch in her hand. Pamela was a sophomore, new to both the team and swimming. Ruth had been swimming her whole life. Pamela was almost at the end of the pool. Ruth swam, struggling as the water pulled her suit, and was easily one length behind. When Pamela's hand touched the edge of the pool, the coach called, "Time—1.02." Pamela had broken her best time by seven seconds.

The next three races—free style, back stroke, and butterfly—pitted a senior in the old uniform against a team member in the new suit. The seniors lost each race. After these four races, the coach clapped her hands. All the girls went into the locker room while the coach wrote the times on a blackboard. In less than two minutes, the teams returned. All the girls were wearing the new formfitting uniforms.

Walter, Virginia, Josephine and Nora Ann jumped up with the rest of the crowd and cheered. The team bowed. Pamela grabbed her book, held it high and waved at the crowd. Walter could not wait to talk to Pamela about Annette Kellerman. When Pamela came out of the locker room, she still had Kellerman's *How to Swim* in her hand.

As she approached, Walter took his sweater, and laid it out on the ground like a cape. "Miss Pamela, please let me protect your Olympic swimming feet, and that wondrous book in your hand."

Pamela already had a soft place in her heart for Walter. She honored him with a movie star smile, tousled his hair with her free hand, and stepped gracefully on the sweater. "Well, Sir Walter, I always love your help. Is there anything I can do for you this fine evening?"

"Well, Miss Pamela, I am curious about the passage you read to the team before today's meet. As a writer, I want to be able to tell the story of our new Coach Jensen and the swim team."

Pamela listened and began to thumb through the book. She did not turn to the bookmarked page, but finally found what she wanted.

"Walter, I believe Miss Kellerman is speaking to you, and I quote:

The way in which literature does not appreciate swimming surprises me. Poets have pushed the subject far away from them, even those who loved it. Lord Byron, who swam the Hellespont, barely mentions the fact. I only wish I could turn all this into poetry, but I can only tell in a faulty way what a glorious human experience it is."

Walter stood taller with each word Pamela read and replied. "Miss Kellerman needs a poet or writer to put swimming on the page. Well, I am her man—and of course I am your man as well. Let me walk all you lovely ladies back to your cottage. Perhaps at lunch tomorrow, you could share what you read to the swim team today."

As promised, Walter and Pamela had their heads together all through lunch the next day— talking and then looking at photos in the book. Pamela gave Walter the book to take to the library and showed him the passage she read the previous night. Walter would be her poet.

***

Later that week, Betty, Pamela, Josephine, and Virginia went to chapel. Walter met them on the way, and immediately gave Pamela her book. As they entered, Mr Harris appeared and motioned Walter aside. After a minute, Walter handed a sheet of paper to Mr Harris. Mr Harris whispered to Walter, Walter considered his words, and then faced Mr Harris with a smile and a nod as Mr. Harris returned the paper.

Mr Harris motioned to Pamela who joined Walter and him as they walked toward the pulpit. They sat in the front pew, where Mr Harris continued to talk to

Pamela until the organ sounded the beginning of chapel. Walter still held the paper in his hand.

As the organist played, Doctor Wesler walked up the chapel aisle with the Bible in his hand. He went to the pulpit, said the evening prayer, and opened the Bible. "Our reading this evening is from the book of Acts, Chapter 3, verses 6 to 8—the story of the lame beggar at the door: *Then Peter said... rise up walk. And he took him by the right hand and lifted him up, and immediately his feet and ankle bones received strength. So, he, leaping up, stood and walked and entered the temple with them—walking, leaping, and praising God.*"

Doctor Wesler held up the Bible. "The Good Book tells stories that make us both kind and strong. It is the best book to do this. There is no better story than the lame beggar who is healed and entered the temple walking, leaping and praising God.

"Mr Harris and I have talked about all the books he hopes to offer in our library. He has convinced me that tonight, instead of a sermon, we would be inspired by a second reading from a very good book by Annette Kellerman. This book belongs to our dear Pamela Duke. I have asked her to read the passage she shared with her team before our last girls' swim meet."

Pamela looked like a queen as she approached the pulpit. She carried *How to Swim*. When she passed the

Captain of the boys' swim team who was seated in the row to her right, she nodded. She stood at the pulpit, opened the book, looked at the congregation and gave a movie star smile. Her royal voice and expression turned every eye her way. She read:

The old days of my crippled childhood seem unbelievably distant as I write this. My early physical misfortune has turned to be the greatest blessing that could have come to me. Without it I should have missed the grim struggle upward and the reward that waited at the end of it all.

I first loved the ocean when I was a child because it made me curious. I wondered whether it really went down and down if it would hold me up. I wanted to know what made it blue and to feel the white on a wave... I have been asked ten thousand times why I like to swim, and I have given a different answer every time. You see the water always teaches me a new story. It is three times as large as the land and too big to be disturbed.

Pamela looked up and smiled. She dramatically closed the book, nodded, and slowly walked back to the first row.

The silence was broken as Walter stood up, shook hands with Mr Harris, and bowed slightly to Pamela. As he walked up to the pulpit, he unfolded the paper in his hands.

"I, too, have been inspired by our swim team and the life of Annette Kellerman. With the encouragement of my dear friends, Josephine and Virginia, and Mr Harris, I have written this poem." Walter looked at the podium for a moment, and then without ever looking down again recited his poem from memory:

Endless
By Walter Raleigh Duke, Dedicated to Pamela Jane Duke

Ocean waves will soothe, but I cannot move
The white of the wave surely my salve
But the journey is endless, endless.
I stretch then I crawl, the crash is my call
To swim, to swim, to swim
But the journey is endless, endless
Time like the sea, seems nothing to me
I will stroke, I will kick, I will speed
But the journey is endless, endless

Josephine could only see Pamela's back. She was not surprised to see her shoulders shaking. Mr Harris moved closer and patted her back. When Walter returned, she looked up at him, and he could see she was crying. She gave Walter both of her hands as he sat down.

A small sound of clapping hands began from the back of the chapel and crescendoed into a rhythmic sound as every student joined in. Doctor Wesler walked to the front of the chapel and whispered to the organist who began to play an old hymn familiar to most of the students and faculty. Doctor Wesler raised his hands and led everyone in song—the singing becoming endless waves of harmony.

As I went down in the river to pray
Studying about that good old way
And who shall wear the starry crown,
Good Lord, show me the way!
O sisters, let's go down,
Let's go down, come on down, O sisters, let's go down
Down in the river to pray,
O brothers, let's go down
Let's go down, come on down, brothers, let's go down
Down in the river to pray

Everyone in the chapel had gone to the river. They felt the water and believed they could swim their cares away. They became both the leaping beggar and swimmers lost in the water's majesty.

During the singing, Pamela and Walter returned to sit with Josephine and Virginia. Doctor Wesler walked down the center aisle, and the students followed row by row. When the singing ended, no one spoke as they walked to their cottages.

Josephine was almost asleep when she felt someone shake her shoulder. She opened her eyes to find Pamela kneeling by her bed with a paper in her hand. "Here is my creed. I will never feel stronger than I do tonight. I want you to have it. I love you, Josephine. You are right. I do wear silky gloves." She put the paper in her sister's hand and went back to bed.

Josephine woke up with the first glint of light— Pamela's paper still in her hand. No one was up as she read...

The Silky Gloves Creed

I, Pamela Jane Duke, believe that sadness lives underneath my skin, and seeps into my mind when I least expect it.

THAT when I feel the sadness, I protect others by wearing silky gloves.

THAT silky gloves keep the sadness in and let me touch others.

THAT when I am in the water and swimming with all my might, the sadness drowns, and joy springs up.

THAT joy and sadness live together, and I must find more keys to joy.

THAT some people are keys to sadness, and some keys to joy.

AND my sadness came the day I was born, not the day my mother died.

Signed, Silky Gloves, June 1921

Josephine felt the tears on her cheeks and understood why Betty had cried the night she read Pamela's creed. She rejoiced for the swim team and hoped that all her life Pamela would be able to swim and find keys to joy.

Chapter 15: Letters

I wondered why my mother and father never saved letters. They would read a letter, talk about it, and in time write a letter to the sender. They did not keep letters. We had no time worn envelopes, stuffed with pages read and reread over the years. Nothing was tied with ribbon for generations to come. You could not find an old stamp anywhere.

I lived on the same street from the time I was two years old. As a child, I never needed to write a letter. I only had one grandparent and I visited her often. She didn't write letters. My aunts called on the phone.

When I went away to college, I wrote letters to my boyfriend. When we broke up, I tore up all his letters. I realized that tearing up a letter makes you feel better for the moment, but the memory of the letter's message will be with you always. I could not rely on my parents' letters for this story. But I can always rely on my memories to recreate a letter.

Josephine sat at the desk in Nora Ann's apartment. She took out a large worn envelope and placed it on her lap. She searched the desk for a pen, stationery and an envelope. She was ready to write to Cleophas, but first removed a worn letter from the large envelope. It was a letter she always read when she wanted to clear her mind. It was the first letter she ever received from Mrs Stevens. The envelope was filled with letters from Mrs Stevens, but this was the one that proved you could say goodbye and still be friends forever.

June 13, 1921

Dear Josephine,

Thank you so much for your beautiful letter. I have a special box for my treasured letters— those from my parents, Doctor Stevens, and all the letters Miss Coffee and Reverend Miller wrote about the wonderful Duke sisters. I hope we will write for many years, but I want to do my very best writing on our first letter.

Doctor Stevens advised me to always: "Begin with your most important idea." Josephine, I love your Iron Pants Creed. I would have loved it even if I didn't know you. But knowing you magnified the power of your creed. It takes talent to write a creed, but living a creed changes the lives of all those around you. You have changed my life and I would like to take the words of your creed and explain how you did this.

I never knew that girls were allowed to fight until I met you. Like all important lessons, I did not like learning it. For a little girl, you were a formidable fighter. I learned that love is not the only thing you need in family life. You need courage. Fighting gives you courage. Thank you.

One of the saddest, and best lessons, I learned from you was learned too late to help me with you and your sisters. I never answered a question that I know you asked Miss Coffee. Why didn't we want to take all four sisters in our home?

Please know that I beg your forgiveness, as I begin. I still had button eyes and could not see. When I was talking to my family and friends about your family, they cautioned that older girls would need to enter the social circles of "our society" very quickly. While your sisters were "pretty enough," my fine family and friends determined that they would not have the social standing or proper training to be successful in their search for a place in a "good family." The advantage of "little girls" was they could be taught our social expectations and Southern code. They felt this would be impossible for older girls.

This terrible advice cost me dearly. I have vowed it will never again cost me children. Our new family is a joyful gift from God. Anyone who doesn't know this is clearly a "Bible-thumper" not one who lives the Loving Word. I know that Reverend Miller and Miss Coffee have told you about our new family. I have enclosed a picture of the four boys for you to share with your sisters.

As you say in your creed, you can live in the South and learn not to be "the South." As soon as we learned that four boys needed a home, we promised ourselves that the advice of family and friends do not reflect the goals we have for a new family.

When we said goodbye at the train station, I knew you meant it when you said you loved us. As you say in your creed, "You can leave someone and still love them very much." As Doctor Stevens and I begin to pack up and leave Asheville, we hope our Southern code family and friends know that we still love them.

I will write you more about our new home and Doctor Stevens' clinic when we get established in Warren County. We can't wait for the four Stevens brothers to meet the four Duke sisters.

Love and happy birthday! Sarah Stevens

Josephine looked at the hand worn photo enclosed in the letter. Doctor and Mrs Stevens were seated on the flowered loveseat in the sitting room where the Strawman learned to see. Doctor Stevens held twin boys that were a year old, John and James. Mrs Stevens held two-year-old Mark on her lap and had her arm around a four-year-old Matthew. There were books on the love seat and blocks all over the floor. The boys all had dark eyes and hair. Matthew was looking at Doctor Stevens and they were both making a funny face. Mrs Stevens and Mark were laughing at the funny faces.

Josephine knew how much these boys were loved and imagined their move to a new healthcare clinic not thirty miles from where she grew up in Warren County. She guessed that they would never become threadbare poor like their neighbors, but she knew their refined Asheville lifestyle had ended. Mrs Stevens did know what to do with all the girls' clothes and fancy little bedroom. She sold them and bought a simple house in the mountains of rural Warren County.

Josephine prayed that each year Doctor Stevens practiced, traveling in his aging motorcar to rural homes, a mother would be saved. In the future, Doctor Stevens would not arrive too late for someone's mother. Josephine folded the letter, carefully placed the photo inside and returned it to the large envelope.

Mrs Stevens' letter had forever changed Josephine's understanding of how life provides opportunities to grow and flourish. It also made her understand that just as she could help people change for the better, she could also make them change for the worse. She hoped she would never do that. She wanted to make sure that all those she loved would benefit from her care. She didn't know why she was thinking of love when she began to write her first letter to Cleophas, but she was.

June 13, 1941
Dear Cleophas,

I have a rule about letters. I always start with my most important idea. This explains why it has taken me a whole week to write to you. I had to make sure I knew what I wanted to say. So here I go...

Nora Ann told me the story of your mother, Sarah, naming you Cleophas. I have read that portion of the Easter story many times, but never noticed the name of the second man on the road to Emmaus. Thanks to your mother, this verse will always be special.

As you might have guessed, family is very important to me—maybe more so than most, because we lost our parents at such a young age. I want you to tell me all about your family in your first letter.

Nora Ann has told you a little bit about our youth and experiences in the Appalachian Jackson Orphanage. Just as your mother used the Good Book to name her children, the Bible was part of every day of our lives at the orphanage. We got religion at breakfast, lunch and dinner and in between. Happily, we also had teachers who respected children. They knew that if they wanted our love and trust, they better be honest.

Throughout our lives, we met wonderful people that we keep in touch with. I was just reading a letter from one of these ladies—Sarah Stevens. Sarah and her husband Matt now live in Warren County, North Carolina, where I was born. She reminded me of something I wrote in fifth grade. I would like to share it with you.

If this doesn't scare you away, I can expect a letter soon. If it does scare you, better we part ways. I don't think I will change. Let me introduce you to Iron Pants—a name I gave myself when our mother died. This is my creed written at the age of ten. I have done some editing, but I still think it describes me to a "T."

The Iron Pants Creed

I, Josephine Helen Duke, believe that I will flourish and thrive because I know:

THAT I will fight, and fight, and fight, until my heart says STOP.

THAT I live in the South, but I am NOT the South.

THAT I will be careful of those who thump the Bible, and respect those who live it.

THAT people can leave you, and still love you very much.

THAT there are many ways of telling the truth, but I prefer to tell it using a story.

THAT singing is a way to lull you into change or accepting the hardest truths.

THAT if you ever have to make a choice about people, stick with your family. They might not be perfect, but they are your family for a reason. Honor them.

THAT sometimes you need to use honey, and not vinegar to get your way. Signed Iron Pants, fifth grade.

I hope I get a letter. I want to know more about you and your family. I will be back to visit Nora Ann before school starts and hopefully, we can eat and laugh some more.

Sincerely, Josephine

P.S. I am using Nora Ann's address since I will be here for another ten days. Not sure how long it will take to hear from you.

Josephine folded the letter, addressed and stamped the envelope, walked to the post office and mailed it. As she walked home, she began to have regrets. Why was she always so honest with those she suspected she might learn to love? The chance of getting a letter from this handsome soldier seemed slim.

June 15, 1941
Dear Josephine,
I want to follow your letter rule and begin with my most important ideas. First, you can't scare me away. I must call my older sister "Major" because she outranks me. I love women who speak their minds. My other idea is that I will never write as beautifully as you, and I will always admire your fine ideas. I hope you will see the truth in my humble writing. I am a simple man.

Now, I must ask you a question. Did you really write to me on your birthday and not mention this most important idea? I saw Nora Ann at the hospital when I was delivering a new ambulance. She told me June 13 was your birthday. She also broke all the rules of the women in my family and told me your age. I love older women.

I am posting this letter immediately. I will be in Washington before you leave for North Carolina. We can eat and laugh some more. I will call Nora Ann to set up a time and place.

Love, Cleo

P.S. Honey always works better with me than vinegar. Xx00

Josephine finished writing her letter. She loved Cleophas' letters and answered them as soon as they arrived. She had sent him a photo of her standing by the mailbox of her boarding house. She spent a lot of time getting dressed for the photo taken by her fellow teacher, Ruth Stedman. Her dark green felt hat framed her face and matched the belt of her soft brown woolen dress. She wore a new coat with a wide rabbit fur collar. Her black purse matched her medium high pumps and like any proper lady, she had gloves. The best part of the picture was her smile. Ruth had commanded, "Say Cleophas!" before she snapped the photo. Cleo's last letter teased her, saying that he had captioned the photo— "Josephine waiting for my letter—I hope!"

Josephine had many men who took her dancing, walking and to dinners. She had even met the parents of one of her "gentlemen callers" but had never found the man for her.

The Cherokee County School System encouraged female teachers to remain single. Married women had to resign as soon as the school year ended. Cleo might be worth looking for a new job. She reread his last letter.

October 15, 1941

Dear Josephine,

Your letters are the most wonderful "care package" any soldier could receive. The picture of you by your landlord, Mr Smith's mailbox is a treasure that I carry with me always. I have captioned it, "Josephine waiting for my letter— I hope!"

I was so interested in your story of the Duke sisters reuniting with their stepbrothers as adults. Betty certainly worked hard to find Robert Duke. You convinced me I missed a great time when you, Betty and Nora Ann met Robert Duke and his wife in New York for the 1939 World's Fair. I have never been to a World's Fair, but I am still young.

Now that I stop and think, I am really a year older today. I almost did what you did in your first letter. Today is my birthday. I think we have established a tradition of writing to each other to celebrate a new year. In fact, I will make a birthday wish that you and I travel together to the next World's Fair. How does this sound to you?

What about being the first person to wish each other Happy Birthday for the rest of our lives? That may sound like a proposal, and I think it is. I need to see you.

Love, Cleo

P.S. My thoughts are with your stepbrother Robert in the Pacific. One of my high school friends is in the Navy and deployed at Pearl Harbor. As we discussed, there is great irony in calling any war the one that will end all wars. We will all need iron pants in the coming months.

Chapter 16: Doctor Wesler

Washington DC
June 1941

Josephine's mind flashed to her small classroom in Cherokee County, North Carolina. She had been reading a world history book to her fifth-grade class for the two months before school ended. The book featured a Staircase of Time beginning with the Stone Age and ending at the beginning of the 20th Century. From the beginning of the Iron Age, most chapters included an announcement of impending war, details of gory battles, or long overdue armistices. She remembered taking the book from her desk, nodding to the children to sit and listen, and opening to the bookmarked page.

One of her favorite students, a dark eyed Cherokee boy named Paul who had listened to each chapter with rapt attention, laughed at the sight of the book. "I bet this new war will be exciting. And I wonder how many will die in the biggest battle."

You could not study history without encountering war. She thought of the many discussions of peace on earth when she was a student at the Appalachian Jackson Orphanage. The orphanage Superintendent, Doctor Wesler, spoke often of war. Then unbidden Doctor Wesler's voice rang in her ears. She was not in the Union Station, but back in the North Carolina orphanage. It was Christmas Eve.

Appalachian Jackson Orphanage
December 24, 1923

The Reverend Martin Luther Wesler was a tall man with round wire glasses, short gray hair, and a very proper white shirt, blue tie and three-piece gray tweed suit. When he read from the scriptures, he seemed to know the words by heart. Fifteen-year- old Josephine liked Doctor Wesler because he had two voices, and two faces. The first Doctor Wesler was the orphanage administrator and preacher that needed to save everyone in the place. His weapons for salvation were lots of scripture references, and boring details about church teaching. The second Doctor Wesler was a North Carolina storyteller. It was the storyteller she loved. Tonight, she needed the storyteller to create some joy this Christmas Eve.

As Doctor Wesler watched from the scratched oak podium in the chapel, students and teachers settled and raised their eyes to him. He cleared his throat and began.

Josephine rejoiced as she listened. He didn't look at the Bible as he proclaimed: *Glory to God in the highest, and on earth peace among men in whom he is well pleased.* He began telling his story:

Doctor Wesler's Sermon on Peace and War

We all long for peace, but we have war. My father and older brothers fought in the Confederate Army during the Civil War—even after Mother begged them not to go. She said she could not run a farm with little children—she meant me and my twin sisters. We didn't own slaves and never would. My mother knew that God was pleased with my father and older brothers. She believed that her men deserved peace on this earth and should not go to war.

I was with my mother when she got the letter that told her both of my brothers were killed in the battle of Gettysburg. They were part of Pickett's charge under the command of Brigadier General Joseph R. Davis— the famous tar-heels of North Carolina. They had been fighting for two days when they made the charge up Cemetery Hill. In the years after the war, my mother always said any soldier should think twice about charging anything with the word cemetery in it. Half of the boys and men that charged that hill died. Mother never said a good word about General Lee because he gave the order that caused my brothers' deaths. When I asked her to explain tar-heel, she said it was because the soldiers of North Carolina stuck to their work as if they had tar on their heels. It is either a compliment, or a sign that they were too stubborn to listen, she said.

Doctor Wesler paused and adjusted his glasses:

When my father learned of my brothers' deaths, he asked if he could return home. His commander said the only way to return home was to desert the army. "You can join the other cowards who are disappearing daily," he said. Father said he was not a coward, but a family man whose wife needed him. He did not leave and wrote Mother every day. Three months after Gettysburg, my father died. They found him dead on his cot in the field office tent. I never thought my mother would recover from her heartbreak. I was only ten, but I knew I had to step up and become the man of the house. My mother and sisters needed me.

I worked with my mother and sisters on the farm. My dreams of an education waited as I took care of my family and we worked to honor the memory of our father and brothers. Finally, my sisters married, and they took control of the farm. My mother had grandchildren to adore, and I was able to fulfill my dream of getting an education.

I wanted to teach children who had lost parents to wars and other evils beyond their control. I was a tarheel for children and their right to go to school and know that they were loved even when those they loved were taken from them.

Doctor Wesler stopped and wiped his eyes. Josephine was lost in his story. Then, without warning, the first Doctor Wesler returned. His voice changed. He was all business:

When I attended the first White House Conference on Children and Youth in January of 1919, a great war had just ended. President Wilson called the conference to arouse the nation on the importance of conserving childhood—especially in times of national peril.

After the war, the nation turned to its children. I continue to represent and honor the children who have lost their parents. We want you to not just have a fair chance, but the best chance to succeed in life. We continue to pray for peace on earth, and to provide excellence in education, a homelike environment, and moral direction for all God's children.

Chapter 17: Going to War

Just as my mother did not talk about being an orphan, I realized that no one ever talked about World War II in our family or community. No one ever spoke of the war years—only the rebuilding of life and family after the war. I found myself returning to the relentless child who wanted to know all about the war years. What happened during the war that no one wanted to remember?

Then I heard my mother's voice cautioning, "Be careful what you wish for…"

Davis Townsend School
Cherokee County North Carolina
December 1941

Josephine and her fellow teachers sat in front of the radio in their boarding house. As soon as the First Lady of the Land Mrs Eleanor Roosevelt began to talk, a hush fell and without speaking, everyone felt the changes in the air.

Good evening, ladies and gentlemen, I am speaking to you tonight at a very serious moment in our history. The Cabinet is convening and the leaders in Congress are meeting with the president. The State Department and Army and Navy officials have been with the president all afternoon. In fact, the Japanese ambassador was talking to the president at the very time that Japan's airships were bombing our citizens in Hawaii and the Philippines and sinking one of our transports loaded with lumber on its way to Hawaii.

By tomorrow morning the members of Congress will have a full report and be ready for action. In the meantime, we the people are already prepared for action. For months now the knowledge that something of this kind might happen has been hanging over our heads and yet it seemed impossible to believe, impossible to drop the everyday things of life and feel that there was only one thing which was important — preparation to meet an enemy no matter where he struck. That is all over now and there is no more uncertainty. We know what we have to face, and we know that we are ready to face it.

I should like to say just a word to the women in the country tonight. I have a boy at sea on a destroyer, for all I know he may be on his way to the Pacific. Two of my children are in coast cities on the Pacific. Many of you all over the country have boys in the services who will now be called upon to go into action. You have friends and families in what has suddenly become a danger zone. You cannot escape anxiety. You cannot escape a clutch of fear at your heart and yet I hope that the certainty of what we have to meet will make you rise above these fears.

We must go about our daily business more determined than ever to do the ordinary things as well as we can and when we find a way to do anything more in our communities to help others, to build morale, to give a feeling of security, we must do it. Whatever is asked of us I am sure we can accomplish it. We are the free and unconquerable people of the United States of America

To the young people of the nation, I must speak a word tonight. You are going to have a great opportunity. There will be high moments in which your strength and your ability will be tested. I have faith in you. I feel as though I was standing upon a rock and that rock is my faith in my fellow citizens. Now we will go back to the program we had arranged...

Eleanor Roosevelt's radio address to the nation, December 7, 1941.

As soon as the music began to play on the radio, there was a knock on the door. Josephine ran to open it. She was not surprised to see Mr Howard, the school principal. "I need your help in getting the word out that there will be no school tomorrow. Here are the lists of families that have phones. If you can call, I will work with our men with cars to reach the families without phones. We will meet at the school tomorrow morning at ten. This should give us enough time to plan and be ready for the president's message. I will bring the radio. I am sure that tomorrow will change all our lives. Thank you, Miss Duke."

Josephine managed to get in touch with all the families on her list. When they arrived at the school the following morning, Mr Howard greeted them. He and two friends had worked until past ten the previous night. They finished their work by getting up at five that morning. Some families that did not have radios at home begged to come to the school and listen.

They were seated in the desks—some with babies on their laps. Mrs Jones, their boarding house owner, had come over with plates of sandwiches and apples. It was a little after noon when the music was interrupted. They all leaned in as President Roosevelt was introduced and began to speak:

Mr Vice President, Mr Speaker, Members of the Senate,
and of the House of Representatives:

Yesterday, December 7th, 1941—a date which will
live in infamy—the United States of America was
suddenly and deliberately attacked by naval and air
forces of the Empire of Japan...

As the president talked about our diplomatic
relationship with Japan, Josephine looked down at the
photo in her hand. Last night, when Eleanor Roosevelt
spoke of having "a boy at sea on a destroyer," Josephine
could not get her stepbrother, Robert Duke, out of her
mind. Her photo was taken in 1928, two years after her
stepbrother had enlisted in the navy at the age of twenty-
seven. In the photo, Robert stood by his wife Irene, with
his arms around her. His dark blue sailor uniform and
white hat contrasted with Irene's stylish black dress and
loose-fitting beige coat. Irene had told Josephine she
ordered both coat and dress from the Sears catalog.
They had laughed remembering that Eleanor Roosevelt
had talked about ordering a favorite dress from the Sears
catalog.

Robert was amused as they talked about catalog
purchases. When the women looked at him, he took off
his cap. "I try to control this mop of curls with my cap.
Even when it is Navy short, the hair most always wins."
He pulled the cap down and Josephine had snapped the

photo. Robert had reenlisted in 1939 and was now stationed at Pearl Harbor, while Irene lived in Ocean Beach, California, with their children. Robert was currently the Chief Commissary Steward on the *USS Arizona*. Josephine listened for any mention of the *USS Arizona* in the president's speech:

The attack yesterday on the Hawaiian Islands has caused severe damage to American naval and military forces. I regret to tell you that very many American lives have been lost. In addition, American ships have been reported torpedoed on the high seas between San Francisco and Honolulu.

Yesterday, the Japanese government also launched an attack against Malaya. Last night, Japanese forces attacked Hong Kong. Last night, Japanese forces attacked Guam. Last night, Japanese forces attacked the Philippine Islands. Last night, the Japanese attacked Wake Island. And this morning, the Japanese attacked Midway Island.

Josephine looked at the photo and wondered how she could get in touch with Irene. The president's voice did not soothe her fears:

As Commander in Chief of the Army and Navy, I have directed that all measures be taken for our defense. But always will our whole nation remember the character of the onslaught against us.

No matter how long it may take us to overcome this premeditated invasion, the American people in their righteous might will win through to absolute victory. I believe that I interpret the will of the Congress and of the people when I assert that we will not only defend ourselves to the uttermost but will make it very certain that this form of treachery shall never again endanger us. Hostilities exist. There is no blinking at the fact that our people, our territory, and our interests are in grave danger. With confidence in our armed forces, with the unbounding determination of our people, we will gain the inevitable triumph—so help us God. I ask that the Congress declare that since the unprovoked and dastardly attack by Japan on Sunday, December 7th, 1941, a state of war has existed between the United States and the Japanese empire.

Franklin Roosevelt's address to Congress, December 8, 1941

Josephine heard the thunderous applause coming from the Congress. Those in the school room jumped up, clapping and stomping their feet.

Josephine could not move. She knew in her heart that Robert Duke was dead. War would threaten and kill those she loved. She needed to call Nora Ann, talk to

Cleophas, and try and reach Robert Duke's wife. She would stand up and fight. She would teach her fifth graders to stand strong, and she would begin tomorrow.

***

Josephine entered her fifth-grade classroom on December 9th. She was surprised to see all her students present. They were sitting straight at clean desks. The air was filled with a new sense of purpose. She did not waste words. "Tell me what happened on two days ago—December 9th-- and how this will change our lives." Five hands immediately flew into the air.

She called on Ethel, a tall farm girl who was the oldest of eight children. "I think a lot of men and boys are going to leave their families and become soldiers. I think the women and children will be running the farms and writing lots of letters to their fathers, brothers and husbands. It makes me sad and proud at the same time."

"I agree with Ethel. We need to make sure everyone who has to fight has exactly what they need to win the war. We need to pay attention to the president and do what he says. I am not sad. I just wish I was older so I could enlist." John was the youngest boy in his family. He could split wood like a man and idolized his older brothers who ran their wood mill.

Mary was a small Cherokee girl who wore a sack dress that reminded Josephine of her childhood clothing. Mary hardly ever raised her hand, but now she was waving an old photo in the air. "Miss Duke, this is a picture of my grandfather in the War to End All Wars. He and his friends worked with British soldiers in Germany. They became code-talkers. When the Germans found a way to break the British codes, they had my grandfather and his friends to deliver messages in our Cherokee language. No enemy ever broke this code."

Story followed story. After an hour, each child took out a notebook and wrote three questions they had about what war would mean to their family, their school and community, and the United States of America. The students could talk quietly to each other. Josephine walked around the classroom and answered questions. She promised them she would ask Mary's grandfather to come and talk to the class about the Cherokee code-talkers. She told them they would begin writing letters in the classroom so they could keep in touch with anyone who had to leave the community and join the war effort.

After lunch, Josephine sat the children down on a rug in the classroom. They had shared many chapters in the history of the world that began with death and destruction. But they had stayed away from death in their homes and community. Now history was coming into the classroom.

In time she would tell them all about her childhood and maybe read some of the Pencilteers stories, beginning with Thaddeus Beauregard. She would have them tell their own stories of grandparents and influenza, racial hatred and intolerance for native people, and of their family fighting in a new war.

But for today, her story was about being strong. The first thing they had to learn was that they were stronger together. They had to believe they could look death in the eye and still live. They had to know their talents and find talents they did not know they possessed. They had to feel the iron in their veins. She would tell them all about Talent Chapel.

Appalachian Jackson Orphanage
Winter 1921

Walter had an idea. He wanted to give the women's swim team a new name, one fitting their sleek new swimsuit...one worthy of Annette Kellerman. He wanted to call the team Apple Jacks—short for Appalachian Jackson. Virginia had been enlisted to create art to advertise the new name. Walter begged, "Come on Virginia, you know one of your pictures is worth a thousand of my words."

When Virginia asked Walter to give her some ideas, he excused himself and went to the back of the library. He returned carrying a big envelope and dumped its contents on the table. Pictures and real dollar bills spilled out. "I want an original Annette Kellerman One Dollar Bill."

Virginia separated the real dollar bills and began organizing them. Walter continued, "I envision Annette Kellerman, an apple and a team around a pool in the design. Team uniforms are decorated with the words *Apple Jacks* and their swim caps have an apple on the side. I found some pictures of dollars, but most came from Mr Harris' safe."

"Look at the Martha Washington on an 1861 one-dollar silver certificate and the 1865 twenty-dollar bill with Pocahontas." Virginia and Josephine marveled at the Pocahontas bill that pictured her baptism. Pocahontas wore a gown and knelt on a podium before a priest. She was flanked by settlers on one side and American Indians on the other.

Virginia took the Pocahontas bill. She nodded as Walter brought her pencils and a pad. Walter and Josephine watched a rectangular shape with a white border and intricate ocean waves appear. Soon *Appalachian Jackson Orphanage, 1920- and One-Dollar Silver Swim Certificate* garnished the top and bottom of the bill. An intricate "1" indicated the dollar amount in each corner. Then Miss Kellerman appeared wearing the Kellerman swimsuit. Across the pool from her stood a swimmer who looked like Pamela—wearing the exact same suit. Apple trees surrounded them on the bill. Two small children, one the image of Nora Ann, were playing jacks under an apple tree.

***

After dinner that night, Walter and Nora Ann stood up in the dining hall. Walter announced that he and Nora Ann would like to teach the swim team fans some new cheers, songs and chants. He asked all the members of the high school swim teams—both men's and women's—to stand.

To Walter's surprise, Miss Faircloth stood up with the teams. She raised her hand, "I know that Walter and Nora Ann have worked hard on these cheers. I also know that many of you need to finish your homework before chapel. If you need to return to your cottage to complete your work, you may leave now."

Josephine was glad she had finished her homework before dinner. She had been thinking about how easy it was for the Pencilteers to do their homework and other class assignments. Some fifth graders were still learning to read and once she heard a boy talk about Walter's "highfalutin' words." She knew that not everyone would be able to cheer the teams to victory. She also knew not to tell Walter, or he would want to ban all homework during swim season.

After more than half the students left, Nora Ann and Walter stood side by side and belted out a song that Walter knew from attending baseball games. The words had changed:

> *Take me out to the swim meet,*
> *Take me out with the crowd;*
> *Look at the swimsuits and Apple Jacks,*
> *I don't care if I never get back.*
> *Let me root, root, root for the girl's team,*
> *If they don't win, it's defeat.*
> *For it's one, two, three strokes, you win,*
> *At the old swim meet.*

Walter and Nora Ann held up a big sign with the new words to the familiar tune. Walter urged everyone to sing along. They did and each time the song became louder and louder.

As Walter raised his hand to lead a third attempt, Pamela and the captain of the Men's Team stood in front of the sign. They motioned everyone to get up and then join hands as they sang. Josephine smiled and noticed that the Men's Team Captain enjoyed the handholding with Pamela as much as the singing.

Walter took advantage of the mood. He held up a picture of the new Annette Kellerman dollar bill. Nora Ann matched Walter's gusto as they chanted:

A dillar, a dollar, Apple Jacks, Holler!!
Swim for the glory, swim for the gold
We're number one—victorious, strong and bold.

Women in the swimming pool, women on our bill
Women at the voting booth, future as they will
Swim for the glory, swim for the gold
We're number one—victorious, strong and bold.

Walter ended by reminding everyone to come to the women's swim meet the following evening. He promised he would have copies of all the new cheers posted near the pool. He also promised a new Kellerman dollar for the class with the most members attending the meet.

Pamela sauntered over to Walter and crushed him with a hug. "Walter, you sure do accomplish what you set out to do. You will inspire our Apple Jacks to gold medals. We will be number one—and not just on a dollar bill!" The captain of the men's team shook

Walter's hand and then grabbed Pamela's hand as they left for chapel.

***

The next afternoon, Walter and Mr Harris had their heads together. There was a big box in the back of the library that had a return address of Atlanta, Georgia, on the side. Eventually, Walter called Virginia and Josephine over. "Mr Harris and his fine mother have just provided the Apple Jacks the missing jewel in their winning crown. Have you ever seen the *Esty Portable Preacher's Organ*?" Virginia and Josephine shook their heads no. "Well, here we go. Mr Harris on the count of three—one, two, three…"

Walter and Mr Harris lifted the box and a small wooden pump organ appeared. Mr Harris stepped up to the keyboard and began to pump the foot pedals and play *Take Me Out to the Swim Meet*. Virginia and Josephine stood open-mouthed.

Virginia found her voice first. "Mr Harris, I want to write your mother a letter and thank her. Would it be all right if I drew a picture of you and Walter by the organ? I am sure she would like to see you in your library."

"That would be lovely, Virginia. I have written Mother about the Three Pencilteers. Could you draw all four of us?" Mr Harris can't finish a question without a little bow.

Josephine took paper and pen from Mr Harris. "Virginia, you begin the illustration and I'll write the letter to Mrs Harris. I think I can find her address on the side of this box!"

In less than an hour, Walter and Mr Harris had moved the portable organ to the chairs near the end of the pool. Virginia's drawing captured the Three Pencilteers flourishing pens and brushes behind Mr Harris as he sat at the organ. The bookshelves and library tables completed the cozy scene. Walter, Virginia and Josephine signed the thank-you letter, and Mr Harris added his own P.S. thanking his mother.

The organ playing and singing at the next night's swim meet inspired the Apple Jacks. Coach Jensen greeted Walter and Nora Ann before the meet and shook their hands. Each swimmer beat their best record in each heat. The junior class won the Apple Jack Dollar with a little more than half their class attending and cheering madly.

Attendance stayed steady and the Apple Jacks began each swim meet with Coach Jensen greeting first the team and then Walter and Nora Ann who led the singing and cheers. Mr Harris belted out *Take Me Out to the Swim Meet* on the organ and improvised tunes for some of the new cheers.

Pamela was the happiest her sisters had ever seen her. She was finding joy at almost every turn in her life. The captain of the Young Men's Swim Team now had a name—Timothy John Wilson. When Pamela wasn't in the pool or class, she was reading or talking about swimming. Timothy loved talking about swimming and found inspiration holding Pamela's hand while they talked.

With her new friends, Josephine shared Pamela's happiness and basked in her own. As she and Virginia were working in the library the last week of March, Nora Ann burst through the library door and screamed, "Where is Walter? I need big brother. I might have to punch that new kid right in the face. What a meanie!"

Josephine reached for Nora Ann's hand. Nora Ann stiffened and screamed louder, "I want Walter. Now!"

"Before we find Walter, you need to tell me what happened. Calm down and tell me who was mean." Virginia left the library in search of Walter.

"Well, I was practicing my Apple Jack cheers and one of the new cottage boys told me to 'shut up.' I told him he was rude, and he said I was a smarty pants."

Walter and Virginia returned together. Walter almost ran over to Nora Ann. "Who called you a smarty pants? Where is he?"

Josephine looked at Virginia who whispered, "I'll go get Mr Harris."

"Nora Ann let's talk to Mr Harris first," Josephine said as she took Nora Ann by the shoulder.

"No, I want Walter to punch him now!" Nora Ann was pulling on Walter's hand and then got behind him and tried pushing him out the library door just as Virginia returned with Mr Harris.

They sat at the library table and Nora Ann told her story to Mr Harris. "One of the new cottage boys saw me cheering and said I was a smarty pants. And then his friend said that all my sisters and their friends were smarty pants, too. They said they would go to watch the swim meet, but they had to do their 'book learning' that they hate. Who hates books?"

Nora Ann caught her breath. Walter tapped his foot and clenched and unclenched his fists. Walter lived in the new boys' cottage and could guess who had tormented Nora Ann.

Mr Harris took Nora Ann's hand and smiled at the Pencilteers. "Nora Ann, I am sorry this happened to you. I will speak to Mr Smith who is the cottage parent for the new boys. We do not expect any student at Appalachian Jackson Orphanage to be unkind.

"I wish I could promise you that this will not happen to you again, but I can't. Sadly, the one thing I have learned is that not everyone likes school and not everyone admires those who do. Being someone with good grades and extra credit does not endear you to those who struggle with books and lessons.

"It doesn't mean that you are right, and others are wrong. It just means that everyone has their own talents. Maybe it means we need a way to tell everyone that there are many ways 'to love the Lord.' I will talk to Doctor Wesler about this. Do not worry. Does this make you feel better?"

Nora Ann smiled. "Pamela loves the Lord when she swims. Walter and I love the Lord when we cheer. Virginia and Josephine make books. We all love the Lord. Amen!"

Walter laughed. "Nora Ann, remember that Sir Walter will always be here, and so will Virginia, Mr Harris and your sisters. You are a very lucky girl. Some of the new boys and girls feel alone and sad. These are the boys where I live and sleep. I will find out more and we will do something!"

***

Josephine and Virginia met Walter in the library the next afternoon. Mr Harris greeted them and left, saying he had a meeting with Mr Smith and Doctor Wesler. "I'll be back soon. I'm sure you can guess what my meeting concerns." They nodded. "See if you can come up with an idea to build a team with the new boys—scholars *and* those who hate books."

Walter took a list from his pocket. He had written the names of each boy in his cottage. "I can't get Mr Harris' words out of my mind—that we all have different talents that should be respected. Maybe we need to stop talking about academics and swimming and find more talents."

Josephine remembered Miss Coffee talking about her brother's work in the orphanage carpenter shop and how she still had a footstool he made. "How do we do this, Walter?"

Walter pointed to his list, "We need to find the talent and something each boy can show or do because of the talent." Virginia and Josephine looked at the list where Walter had written, *Walter: poetry and cheers*.

Josephine looked at the other eleven names. "Can we write what we think, or should we ask each boy? I think we know some of this already."

Virginia continued, "We need to be especially careful that we get the talents of the boys who bothered Nora Ann. They can't be left out again or they will really hate us. Let's fill in what we know and then find time to talk to the other boys. We can get this done today."

Josephine picked up Virginia's thoughts, "I want to talk to the boys who work in the carpentry shop. I'll start by telling them about my daddy and all the things he made. I bet they have things to show me." Virginia had two boys that she had watched in chapel she would talk to at lunch. They agreed to meet before chapel and complete the list.

***

Josephine and Virginia looked at Walter's finished talent list.

Walter: poetry and cheers

Robert: rope making; piece of hemp rope made at farm by Robert and his uncle

James: singing; demonstration of singing favorite hymns

David: dancing; demonstration of square dancing

Daniel: swimming; come see him on the swim team

Jacob: whittling; a robin he made from a walnut tree at his home

Mark: fishing; using some of Robert's rope and a hairpin, he fashioned a fishing pole from a stick found near the cottage

Luke: preaching; three Bible verses on using talents

John: fighting; demonstrated how to stand and knock your opponent's teeth out

Zachariah: joke-telling; three farmer jokes

Joseph: woodworking; a tray he had made at home in his father's shop

Phillip: knitting from homemade yarn; a hat his mother taught him to make

The Pencilteers' proposal was simple. Talent Chapel would highlight the talents of the new boys' cottage. The service would begin with James leading the singing. Luke would follow reading his scriptures from Exodus and Proverbs. Instead of a sermon, the other boys would show their talent (dancing, boxing, fishing, joke-telling—promised to be Biblically clean and holy) or what they had made with their talent—robin, book, tray and hat. They would end by having everyone in chapel telling the person behind them their talent. James would lead the last hymn and with the help of David, they would all dance out of chapel.

Doctor Wesler beamed when Walter, Virginia and Josephine finished their description of Talent Chapel. He asked how he, Mr Harris and Mr Smith could help. Walter proposed that Mr Smith ask the boys if they liked the idea. Doctor Wesler interrupted, "Why Walter, my lad, you could ask them yourself."

Walter looked down, "I think they might say 'yes' sooner if Mr Smith asked them. You know that I am still a 'highfalutin' bookworm who used to be a rich kid."

Doctor Wesler patted Walter on the back. "We will have Mr Smith work on this. I think he is very persuasive—that's why he is a cottage parent."

Virginia had begun to sketch their next book, "Talent Chapel—singing, fighting, dancing and more." This sketch became the sign that greeted all the students at the Appalachian Jackson Orphanage Chapel as they entered the first Sunday in April.

Talent Chapel with Singing, Fighting, Dancing and More

As the students settled into the pews, they looked up at the pulpit. Twelve boys sat in two rows of six chairs on each side of the altar.

James began the service, "I ask you all to turn to page forty-four in your hymnal. This is a familiar hymn, but I have created a new verse. To help me with this I am asking Nora Ann Duke to come up with the words to our new verse." Nora Ann came with a sign almost as big as she was. She stood in front of the pulpit, put the sign on the floor and held it upright. James continued, "As you can see, our new verse celebrates tonight's chapel theme."

Amazing grace, how sweet thy gift, that made a boy like me!

My talent found, and now profound, I present my gifts to thee.

James sang the words to the new verse. He had a rich voice that spanned three vocal ranges from alto to baritone. When the hymn was over, he motioned for Nora Ann to join him and take his chair. He took the sign, placed it against a wall and stood behind Nora Ann.

When everyone was seated, Luke walked to the pulpit and picked up the Bible. "This is the Good Book and has wisdom for every occasion, every need. When I began to explore God's words on using our talents, I found my answer in Exodus, Chapter 31, verses 3, 4 and 5. Listen and love your talents:

And I have filled him with the Spirit of God, in wisdom, and in understanding, and in knowledge, and in all workmanship, to devise skillful works, to work in gold, and in silver, and in brass, and in cutting of stones for setting, and in carving of wood, to work in all manner of workmanship."

James paused. "And now to the book of Matthew, Chapter 21, verses 12 to 13:

And Jesus entered into the temple of God and cast out all of them that sold and bought in the temple, and overthrew the tables of the money-changers, and the seats of them that sold the doves; and he saith unto them, It is written, My house shall be called a house of prayer: but ye make it a den of robbers."

Luke placed the Bible on the pulpit. "Our first talent demonstrates the wisdom of Jesus in the Temple. I will ask John, our fighter, to take the role of Jesus. Walter, please take your place with the moneychangers and sellers of doves."

Walter moved a table that was covered with dollar bills in front of the pulpit. John slowly approached the table. With lightning speed, he tipped over the table and grabbed Walter by the shirt collar, "Out of our temple, you money grubber. You don't want to find out what a good fighter I am."

The chapel was filled with laughter and clapping. Walter took John's hand, and they took a bow together.

James returned to the pulpit, "Now we will celebrate all manner of workmanship. My fellow cottage mates will tell you about their talents and show you the skillful works they have devised."

Robert held up his rope, "This rope is made from hemp. I made it at my uncle's farm before he passed. He wanted me to take his skills beyond his grave."

Jacob took a knife and wooden robin from a basket, "My father taught all his boys how to whittle. My mother loved her birds and I made this for her before she died. The wood is from a walnut tree that was struck by lightning."

Mark had a fishing pole, "I made this pole from a tree limb I found near the cottage. I was able to use some of Robert's rope for my line and got a hairpin from Miss Faircloth for my hook."

Joseph and Phillip walked up together. Joseph held a wooden tray and Phillip was wearing a woolen cap. Phillip began, "My friend Joseph is as skilled a woodworker as you could want, but he hates to speak in public. I am wearing a hat that I knitted myself. My family raised sheep and mother made yarn before they died."

Daniel and Walter were next and led the chapel in a swim cheer for both poetry and swimming, "Walter is a poet and cheerleader, too. Daniel don't talk but swims 'till he's blue."

Doctor Wesler arranged for the Jokester Zachariah to end the "sermon." Zachariah stood at the pulpit and looked out at those gathered in the chapel. He looked as holy and somber as any preacher.

"How long did Cain hate his brother? As long as he was Abel."

Doctor and Mrs Wesler joined Zachariah at the pulpit when the laugher ended. Doctor Wesler looked at his wife and asked, "My dear, do you know why God created man before woman?"

Mrs Wesler shook her head no.

"So, He wouldn't have to listen to her advice on how to do it." The faculty laughed the loudest. Doctor and Mrs Wesler held hands and bowed.

Doctor Wesler continued, *"My wife and I have never danced before in church. As a matter of fact, I don't think we have ever danced at all. Tonight, I have learned that with new talents come new ideas.*

"So tonight, we will not only sing as we leave chapel, we will dance. To quote the Psalms: Let them praise his name with dancing, making melody to him with tambourine and lyre!

"David and James please come forward. Let's join James in singing our last hymn—a gospel favorite Make a Joyful Noise unto the Lord. *David will lead us as we dance out of chapel. Mrs Wesler and I will follow James and try our best. You may walk or dance—depending on your various talents. And know that unless you try, you might have talents you have not yet discovered."*

Mr Harris played the Esty organ and James' rich voice inspired everyone to sing and follow in the dancing. Josephine was delighted to see that Mrs Wesler was a natural dancer. Dancer David saw this immediately and took Mrs Wesler's hand as they waltz stepped down the aisle. Doctor Wesler followed with a sort of jumpy walk and faculty and students alike did a nice job of swaying and stepping as they sang the hymn and left the church.

Chapter 18: Country Clinic

Appalachian Jackson Orphanage
April 1921

It was in early April that Coach Jensen began to cough. She said it was nothing, but when she coughed up blood, Doctor Wesler immediately called Doctor Stevens. The Sport Touring Roamer arrived with Doctor Stevens behind the wheel the next day. As soon as he saw Coach Jensen and listened to her lungs, he announced that she would be returning with him to the Asheville Clinic. He also said that anyone on the swim team who had persistent cough and fever should immediately be quarantined and to call him.

Before Coach Jensen left, she wrote a note to Pamela asking her to continue the women's swim team training schedule. The men's swim team coach would work with her team to coordinate swim meets. She ended her note with stern advice. "Under no circumstances should my health setback have any impact on our team. The Apple Jacks are going gold."

Betty got permission from Doctor Wesler to ride back with Doctor Stevens to see the Asheville Clinic. She was going to stay for a week and help Mrs Stevens with the four little boys as the family continued their packing.

Nora Ann pitched a fit because she wanted to go in the fancy car. Betty assured her that she could come and visit the Stevenses when they were settled in their new mountain home—within a half day's trip to Appalachian.

Nora Ann stomped out of the cottage and ran into Walter who had come over to say goodbye to Betty. "Well, my little cheerleader, are you thinking we are late for a swim meet? Your sisters are getting their exercise chasing after you."

Josephine nodded at Walter and watched Nora Ann try to enlist Walter in her cause. "I want to go with Betty, but they won't let me. I want to ride in the big car and meet the four little boys. I would be the oldest and not the youngest one for a change!"

Walter saved the day. "But, Nora Ann, what would I do without you? Coach Jensen is leaving, and the team is depending on you and me to keep the Apple Jacks' winning streak going. You can't leave me now. We are a team!"

Nora Ann turned her head, twisted her lips and narrowed her eyes. She considered Walter's words.

Then she sighed and took his hand. "Okay, Walter, I won't let you down. Want to practice our cheers?"

Doctor Stevens returned with Doctor Wesler. Doctor Stevens took Betty's arm, leading her to his car. Doctor Wesler helped Coach Jensen into the backseat. She had a strange mask covering her mouth and nose. Betty and Doctor Stevens sat in the front of the roadster. With more waves and good-byes, they sped down the road to Asheville. The last thing Doctor Stevens did was hand a letter to Josephine.

***

Walter stood in silence as Josephine read her letter from Mrs Stevens. "Josephine, I know how much you love your letters from Mrs Stevens. I am going to find Virginia and see if she can draw a picture of Thaddeus Beauregard to send with your reply to Mrs Stevens' letter. You can tell us all about the clinic today in the library. I sure have some questions for Mr Harris. I think his mother is more generous than we know."

Josephine reread the letter as she sat on her cot.

April 3, 1921
Dear Josephine,
Thank you for the wonderful and heart-breaking story of Thaddeus Beauregard and Mother Bear. I have

only been a mother for two months and I already know how fierce I would be if anyone came after my four boys. I agree that we need to tell honest stories, even if they are sad ones. I also agree that this is not the final victory for T.B.

Reverend Miller and Doctor Stevens spent many hours in university talking about what was needed in the South to make sure that God's work continued. Reverend Miller chose the church and Doctor Stevens, medicine. They agreed that they both wanted to serve the rural poor and help the orphans. After college Reverend Miller jumped right into this work. My husband of course had to get more "facts and friends" before he had a plan. I am sure if we did not have our new family, he would have spent years with his study. Fatherhood changes men immediately.

Our new clinic's name carries the name of our benefactors— James B. Duke and George R. Harris Rural Health Clinic. Lots of money was needed to build a clinic, hire staff, purchase equipment, medicines and so forth. The Duke and Harris families made our dream a reality.

We have sold our house and other property in Asheville. Our new and much smaller house next to the clinic is almost finished. We are equal distance between Appalachian Jackson and Norlina where the Millers will be living. Being as close as we are to Durham, we have the support of the many churches, Trinity College, Lincoln hospital and of course ELECTRICITY. You know how Doctor Stevens loves the "latest" things.

The clinic will have twelve beds and of course our automobile to reach folks who can't travel to us. When the building and house are completed, our "little lights will shine" day and night. We will have photos when we see you on May 5th. Doctor Wesler will bring you and your sisters with him for the wedding on May 4th.

Thank you for "sharing" Betty with our family for the week. Our new house will be smaller than the one you know, but it will always be full of love. Right now, it's all my "earthly possessions" that are giving me a headache. Write soon and as always include stories and pictures.

Love, Sarah, Matt, Luke, Mark, John and James

Chapter 19: I Will and I Do

Blue Ridge Summit Pennsylvania
May 30, 1992

As family and friends gathered at the Hawley Church to celebrate my parents' 50th Wedding Anniversary, I looked out the church window toward the Appalachian Trail. As I watched hikers of all ages pass by at a variety of paces, I realized that this trail passed through North Carolina, Maryland, Pennsylvania, and New York. The story of Josephine and Cleophas' life together blazed a trail through these same states.

Standing by my parents, greeting our guests, I listened as the stories and memories flowed. I noticed that no one told stories about how Mother and Daddy met, or who they had been until they moved into their first home in 1947. This was a celebration of life that began after World War II. No one ever spoke of the war years—only the rebuilding of life and family after the war.

All the stories began with a smile or a wink of an eye toward my parents. Former neighbors, relatives and church friends remembered watching their children play together. They laughed about projects, people, and parties shared over decades of friendship. Everyone agreed that the grandchildren were growing up too quickly. "Time just keeps flying," was heard again and again.

Washington DC
May 1942

Josephine's school year ended in the middle of April. The children were needed to help their families on the farms, and in the shops and factories. Many men had left for the war. Josephine had not submitted a resignation letter to the Cherokee County School Board, but she was sure that she would not be returning.

As she packed to take the train to Washington, DC, Josephine knew t she would be staying in a different apartment. Nora Ann had already left for Texas where she would be stationed. She had given Josephine the name of some friends who had an apartment in the same C Street address where she lived. Cleophas would meet her at Union Station. He was on leave and his last letter said he had news about his deployment.

Josephine was prepared for a formal proposal of marriage. She took her best summer dress and a new hat.

She could not take all her clothes, books and other possessions on this short trip. But she packed as if they would be shipped to her, not stored for another school year.

***

As the train pulled into Union Station, Josephine remembered her visit in 1941 when Nora Ann first introduced her to Cleophas. They had been writing for over a year and saw each other during her school breaks. She had met his older sister and his brothers who were all in the Army and stationed in Virginia and Texas.

When Betty met Cleophas, she told her sister that he was a man their mother would have loved. She also said that Cleophas could have carried on a conversation with anyone who lived in Warren County or in the Zion Church.

Josephine got her bag and suitcase and adjusted her hat as she walked toward the train door. She immediately heard Cleophas' voice, "Josephine, over here." She walked down the ramp and onto the station floor and was in Cleophas' arms in a minute. They walked out of the station, into the waiting room and to the restaurant.

After they placed their dinner order, Cleophas took Josephine's hand, and his face was sober. "Josephine, you know how much I love you. There is no other woman in the world that I would want to marry."

Josephine moved closer and put her hand on top of Cleophas' hand. She was waiting for the proposal but began to see something else in his eyes. She was about to speak when he shook his head. "Josephine, I am about to say the most difficult words I have ever said to anyone. Please hear me out.

"I just got my orders. I will leave for England at the first of the year. I have searched my soul, and I cannot ask you to marry me. I will be in battle, and no one has any idea how long this war will last. It would be irresponsible of me to ask you to be my wife when I do not know if I will be alive in the next year. I do not want you to be a widow. You should be free until we know if I survive the war. I love you too much to make you so uncertain of your future."

Josephine listened and her heart quickened. She understood his words, but she knew her heart. She kissed his hand, "Cleophas, if we do not marry, I know you won't come home from the war. I know that my love will keep you safe. I can stand anything, but I must be your wife—the one who will be waiting to greet you with open arms. You will return to me."

Appalachian Jackson Orphanage
Spring 1921

A big box arrived for the Duke girls at the end of April. It was from Asheville and contained four new dresses— all in different styles and shades of blue. Betty loved her tailored dress with silver buttons on the cuffs and neckline. She told her sisters that while she was in Asheville, she had seen the dress in a store window and had admired it. Pamela's dress had a movie star look with a scooped neckline, full skirt and flowing sleeves. Josephine's was soft at the collar and looked a lot like the old dress she always wore when she'd lived with the Stevenses—the dress her mother had made and mended so many times. Nora Ann's dress was still a frilly little princess style that suited her perfectly.

Josephine asked Walter and Virginia if they could make a copy of their book *Talent Chapel* to give to Reverend Miller and Miss Coffee as a wedding present. It was Josephine's favorite book so far because it had the least number of words and the most pictures. Virginia's illustration of David and Mrs Wesler dancing down the aisle would make anyone smile, they agreed.

The day to travel to Norlina for the wedding arrived with all the glory of spring. The dogwoods were in bloom. Little robins peeked from their nests and a gentle mountain breeze assured the travelers they could leave winter coats and hats at the orphanage.

Josephine hugged Walter and Virginia the night before she left. "We are getting up so early, the four of us are sleeping at the Weslers' house so we don't disturb the cottage when we leave. I will miss my fellow Pencilteers, even if it is only for three days." Walter and Virginia hugged Josephine again and assured her they would be waiting no matter how late she arrived on Monday.

It was still dark on Saturday when the Duke sisters and Doctor and Mrs Wesler left for Norlina. Doctor Wesler had a Chevrolet 490 and Josephine was glad they had blankets on the back seat where she, Pamela and Betty sat. Nora Ann sat between Doctor and Mrs Wesler and was asleep again before they left the orphanage grounds. The older sisters snuggled under blankets and slept when they could.

After driving for six hours with breaks to "run around, visit the bushes, and take a snack from the picnic basket," they arrived in Norlina at the Reilly farm. Josephine noticed Reverend Miller's new horse in the pasture with the Reilly's old, crippled mare.

Reverend Miller had told the girls that the Stevenses had taken money from the sale of one of their properties and bought a roadster for "the newlyweds." Miss Coffee had already learned how to drive it.

Betty had barely finished introducing Doctor and Mrs Wesler to the Reilly family, when Reverend Miller and Miss Coffee drove up in a Roamer. The Millers' car looked exactly like the Stevens'—except theirs was black, not silver, gray.

Mrs Reilly greeted them, "Here you are! Are you ready for a nice country church lunch and practice for tomorrow's ceremony?" Miss Coffee had talked to Mrs Reilly, and they agreed that it might be best for Nora Ann to stay at the farm and not do a rehearsal. As soon as Nora Ann saw the horses, she agreed.

Doctor Wesler shook hands with Reverend Miller and took two sheets of paper from his coat pocket. "Well, my friend, this service is as simple as can be. Are you sure we need to practice? And did you get my letter asking if we could dance out of the church when the ceremony ends?"

The Duke sisters had not been to the Zion Church since their mother's funeral. Reverend Miller said they should come to the rehearsal so they could have time to think about their family. He said they could visit the cemetery if they wanted.

Pamela said the cemetery was not for her. She had her family in her heart and did not need to go backward. She then announced that she had a dancing dress and was all in favor of Doctor Wesler's dancing exit for the wedding. Betty would not visit the graves. Josephine did not know how she would feel until they got to the church.

As the Chevrolet and Roamer drove up the lane to the Zion Church, Josephine remembered the beautiful stones adorning the exterior walls, the bell tower and gracious arched door. The steps to the front door now had a metal railing that she did not remember.

Before they had parked their cars, the sound of the Stevens' roadster was heard on the lane. Betty was out of the car and obviously wanted to hold her "babies" again. She had not stopped talking about how beautiful and smart these four little boys were since her week in Asheville.

Pamela could not wait to thank Mrs Stevens for her dress. Josephine just wanted to see Mrs Stevens in person. They had only been writing letters since she had left Asheville. So much had changed, and she loved Mrs Stevens even more today.

The silver-gray Roamer parked next to her black roadster sister car. Betty opened the front door and took the twins from Mrs Stevens. Mrs Wesler immediately grabbed the hands of the other two boys. Josephine leaned in and hugged Mrs Stevens before she got out of the front seat. Josephine stood back and offered Mrs Stevens her hand. When she was out of the car, Josephine hugged her again. Doctor Stevens shook hands with Pamela and Betty and goofy-faced

Josephine. She goofy faced him back. Mrs Stevens laughed and drew them close in a big hug.

Doctor Wesler greeted the Stevenses and said he thought they could do the rehearsal in less than twenty minutes and then the rest of the afternoon could be for "good eating" and "catching up." He was right. Mrs Wesler played the piano as the bride and groom walked up the aisle. The rehearsal was short, and Doctor Stevens said he would save his words for tomorrow during the real ceremony. Mrs Wesler played *Make a Joyful Noise unto the Lord*, but no one danced down the aisle. They all were headed to the basement where they could smell the wonderful lunch and hear the church ladies humming as they set the table.

***

The wedding was after the Sunday service the next day. The church members were invited, neighbors, college friends and other teachers and clergy. Josephine realized it was mostly members of the congregation who filled the pews. It was still hard for folks to get to the rural community.

Miss Coffee wore a dark green suit, and her hat was a dark brown straw hat with a wide brim and green bow in the back. As she walked down the aisle with Reverend Miller, Josephine didn't see her clothes—just her radiant smile and eyes. Miss Coffee and Reverend Miller had each found their help meet and felt the blessing of their union. Reverend Miller's suit was not new, but it was better than any suit the girls had seen him wearing in a year. Josephine noticed how similar in size Doctor Stevens and Reverend Miller were.

Doctor Wesler read the Bible verse and sat down as Doctor Stevens came up to speak. *"It is good that man shall not be alone; I will make a help meet for him.* When I first met David Miller, we discussed the very God that understood that man should not be alone. I felt alone in the class filled with ministers until I met David. Within an hour, I knew we would always be friends and that I would do anything my friend needed. We agreed about how to serve the God that brought us together.

"I knew the moment I met Sarah that David would also recognize my help meet. David rejoiced with me and served as the best man at our wedding. God needed David to finish his studies and find his mountain flock before he brought Mary to her beloved. David recognized his help meet and so did all of us who loved him. Today I am David's best man and I rejoice with my friend and his new bride.

"God does not stop knowing what you need, and his gifts are as mysterious and holy as God. He finds you friends, communities to use your special gifts, and in time He provides you with family. As I stand here, I rejoice in my family, my dear friends and the wisdom of God. Sarah and I and our four sons will be your neighbors and we will be lifelong friends."

When Doctor Stevens sat down, Mrs Stevens was crying and so were the bride and groom. Doctor Wesler waited for what seemed like a long time before he stood up. The bride and groom stood before their friends and flock and repeated their vows. Reverend and Mrs Miller kissed, and the church organist began to play *Make a Joyful Noise unto the Lord*.

Reverend and Mrs Miller went down the aisle followed by Doctor Wesler. Doctor Wesler stopped at the front pew where Mrs Wesler sat with Pamela. Mrs Wesler stood up, smiled at Doctor Wesler, and then hand-in-hand with Pamela they danced down the aisle. Betty and Josephine followed dancing, with Nora Ann skipping behind. Doctor Stevens had one twin in each arm and Mrs Stevens held two-year-old Mark and four-year-old Luke by the hand, and they followed dancing. The congregation looked at the dancers and then followed suit. They followed the delicious smells to the church basement. The meal was heavenly.

Chapter 20: Mountain Laurel

If someone were to ask which of my mother's stories left the biggest impression on me, I would say the story of my father's proposal. How could my mother lose her parents and still believe that love would protect those that you love? How could she say, "If you marry me, you will come home."?

Blue Ridge Summit Pennsylvania
Winter 1992

Cleophas was keeping a promise he made to his grandson. He was going to let Timothy interview him about the Normandy Invasion. His unit was part of the 11th wave to hit the beaches. He had notes and was waiting for the call. He asked that no one be in the room while they talked.

As Josephine left the room, he called her back. "I hope this doesn't bring back my bad dreams. I don't want you to lose any sleep. Remember you were the one in my thoughts as I hit the beaches of Normandy. Your faith kept me strong."

Zion Church Warren County North Carolina
May 1921

After the wedding and lunch, Reverend and Mrs Miller left for a honeymoon week in Asheville. Some of the boys in the church had tied old cans on the bumper of the car. The Duke sisters loved the racket as the newlyweds drove down the lane.

Pamela and Nora Ann went back to the Reilly's farm with Doctor and Mrs Wesler. Nora Ann's last words were, "teach me that dance."

Betty stayed with Josephine at the church. She did not want to visit graves and her real interest was in playing with the four boys. Doctor Stevens stayed with them, "You are strong, Betty, but this team of four needs us both after all the pie and cookies they had for lunch."

Mrs Stevens took Josephine's hand as they walked to the cemetery. "Do you want me to stay here by the gate and let you be alone?"

"Yes, but please help me pick some Mountain Laurel for my parents' graves. I want to pick a bouquet for you as well."

Josephine gave Mrs Stevens her cluster of Mountain Laurel and hugged her as she entered the cemetery alone. So much had happened since she was last here. In her heart, she knew that she still wanted her mother and father.

Josephine looked back at Mrs Stevens standing in the gateway. She was looking at her flowers with a peaceful smile. A soft spring breeze brought the gentle aroma of honeysuckle as Josephine placed the flowers on her parents' graves. She knew they would leave early in the morning for the orphanage with the Weslers. She knew that Virginia and Walter would be waiting up for her no matter what the time.

"I love you Mother. I love you Daddy." Josephine walked to the gate and Mrs Stevens took her hand. Love and iron flowed in her veins.